MW00625917

Sunsets Never Wait

JONATHAN CULLEN

LIQUID MIND PUBLISHING

All rights reserved. No part of this book may be reproduced, distributed, or transmitted in any form or by any means, including photocopying, recording, or other electronic or mechanical methods, without the prior written permission of the author, except in the case of brief quotations embodied in critical reviews and certain other noncommercial uses permitted by copyright law.

Copyright © 2021 by Jonathan Cullen

www.jonathancullen.com

Liquid Mind Publishing

This is a work of fiction. Any resemblance to actual persons, living or dead, or actual events is purely coincidental.

Also by Jonathan Cullen

The Days of War Series

The Last Happy Summer

Nighttime Passes, Morning Comes

Onward to Eden (Coming Soon)

Shadows of Our Time Collection

The Storm Beyond the Tides

Sunsets Never Wait

Bermuda Blue

The Jody Brae Mystery Series

Whiskey Point

City of Small Kingdoms

The Polish Triangle

Love Ain't For Keeping (Coming Soon)

Sign up for Jonathan's newsletter for updates on deals and new releases!

https://liquidmind.media/j-cullen-newsletter-sign-up-1/

And maybe what they say is true
Of war and war's alarms,
But O that I were young again
And held her in my arms.

— William Butler Yeats

One

IRELAND 1981

A thick mist hung in the air as James Dunford drove the rented Toyota along the narrow road. Hills rose like behemoths on both sides, casting shadows across the valley. To his left was a lake, dark and lifeless, with the remnants of a stone dock. He wondered, as he went, what ancient angler might have fished from those shores, or if there were ever any fish at all. The truth was, no matter how mesmerizing, the landscape of Connemara seemed unfit for habitation, whether bird, beast, or man. It was a vast stretch of rock and shale, as barren as the surface of the moon. For miles at a time, the only signs of life were the endless sheep, their heads down and chomping on the thick, fibrous grasses that had evolved to survive the brutal climate. Jagged stone walls covered the landscape, crisscrossing glens and scaling the hills, the legacy of the mysterious people who first settled the area millennia before.

By the time James came out of the mountains the sun was starting to set. He had another cigarette and stared ahead where, in the distance, he could now see the ocean and the dark shapes of islands offshore. The car bounced over the rough ground, knocking ashes across his lap, and he squinted to see in the ever-diminishing light. He searched for something he recognized—a street sign, schoolhouse, hillock—some unchanged thing that would bring him back to his long, forgotten childhood. James hadn't been to Ireland in three decades and his memories from that time were as scattered as they were hazy. Still, there was something familiar about the place. Maybe it was the scent, he thought, the smoke from burning turf which rose from all the chimneys, sweetening the air like a spring bloom.

James came around a bend and saw a small stone bridge. Before it was a road, little more than a dirt path with grooves made by automobiles and tractors. He turned onto it, following the course of a stream that eventually widened into an estuary. He passed the house where his cousins once lived, now modernized with a corrugated roof and electricity. As a boy, he spent as much time there as he did in his grandmother's house, separated from his relatives by only twenty yards of bogland and scurvy grass. Uncle Franny died from tuberculosis while James was in the service, and his aunt moved to London to live with her sister. Their two children left Ireland the moment they finished school, and the last James heard about his cousins was that Margaret was married with kids in Australia and that Owen was working on oil rigs somewhere in the North Sea.

The road continued to narrow, branches smacking against the side of the car until finally, he reached the cottage, just yards from the shore. He pulled into the yard, shut off the engine, and got out. It was so quiet he could hear his heart beating—so still he could feel his pulse. He looked towards the water, the rugged coastline of rocky headlands and sandy inlets, formed by nature and eroded by time. On a small hill across from the house he saw the shell of an old dwelling, where, as a child, he would play for hours with his cousins, climbing over its moss-covered walls, searching for snakes or pretending to be pirates or soldiers.

James reached in the car for his duffle bag and walked over to the front door. The tidy cottage of his memories was now derelict, its plaster walls cracked in places, the window frames stained with mildew. The property was overgrown with weeds and shrubs, and beside the wire fence, he could see the outline of his grandmother's garden.

He stooped to lift the mat, his back sore from driving, and when he looked underneath, a single copper key lay flat against the cement. He opened the door and was met by a burst of cold, stagnant air. He put down his bag, found a lamp, and when the light came on, he smiled. Except for the décor, it was much how he remembered it. To his right was a kitchenette with a few cabinets, a sink, an icebox, and a range. On the left, a parlor with a tufted couch, coffee table, and a chair in each corner. There was a stone fireplace too, its mantel blackened from years of use, a pile of dried turf in a crate beside it. A short hallway led to the bathroom and two bedrooms in the back, but he didn't have time to look because he needed to get the rest of his things.

James went back out to the car and got his luggage, a large green suitcase with a plastic handle and two buckles. It was as new as the day he bought it at Sears Roebuck back in '67, a set of two that he and his ex-wife got for a vacation to Bermuda. He never got to use it, however, because only two weeks later he called up for deployment.

As he pulled it out, something yelped and he sprung up, hitting his head on the roof. He backed out of the car and turned around to see a dog.

"Goddammit," he said, putting the suitcase down and rubbing his crown.

The animal gazed up, its mouth open and panting in the crisp, evening air. It was thin and mangy, with a yellow matted coat and an ear that looked like it had been mutilated in a fight. James shook his head, as much out of pity as out of disgust, and dragged the suitcase towards the front door. When he heard the pitter-patter of footsteps, he looked back and the dog was following him.

"Go on, boy. Get outta here."

The animal stopped but didn't go away. James took the luggage in and when he came back out, the dog was waiting in the yard. He watched it as he walked over to get the last of his things, a portable Smith Corona typewriter in a black travel case. As he lifted it, a gust came off the water and he felt some raindrops. Worried it might start to rain, he hurried to get back inside, and the dog ran alongside him.

"Scram!"

It looked up and let out a quick, piercing bark. James put the type-writer down and went at it, waving his arms to scare it off. The animal flinched but it didn't cower, and as much as James wanted it to go, he admired its courage. As he knelt to get the typewriter, the dog crept towards him, its head bowed and tail down.

"What is it, boy?"

When it whimpered, James felt some vague compassion which he blamed on hunger and fatigue. But he ignored it, backing into the doorway with the typewriter under his arm, eyeing the animal with a suspicious gaze. It reared towards him suddenly then stopped, and he was prepared to kick it if he had to. In one final plea for attention or shelter, the dog howled and James slammed the door, leaving it to the cold, dark night.

Two

Tara Doherty sat at the kitchen table, sipping tea and nibbling at the courant biscuits she bought in the village a few days before. They were slightly stale, crumbling in her fingers, but she didn't have an appetite. She was irritable from lack of sleep, her neck stiff and her eyes bleary. Somehow, she could tolerate the days, but the nights were agony as she lay tossing in the bed, thinking of Kevin and cursing God for all that happened. She would think about their old life back in London, the long days at work and the evenings spent together where, after a slow meal, they might sit for hours talking in the dim light of their tiny flat. Outside the street bustled with tourists, students, and beatniks. Smells of cumin and paprika rose from the Turkish restaurant below, and the sounds of zithers mixed easily with Led Zeppelin in the vibrant immigrant neighborhood that had been their home for three years. It wasn't that those days seemed like another era—they seemed like the lives of two different people. But she would go back to it in an instant.

Tara turned her head sharply, hurling the memories from her mind so she could brave another day. She reached for the letter from Alice, the few short sentences, the date and time that she wanted to meet in

Galway City. When it arrived a week before, Tara had considered not going. But the problem with living without a phone was that there were no polite declines, no last-minute cancellations. If she didn't show up, Alice would be left waiting, and she couldn't do that to her younger sister.

They hadn't seen each other since the previous fall, a rushed coffee and scone, a conversation that, as always, was disjointed and never quite complete. They had met in Athlone, an hour east of Galway, where Alice was attending a convention for skincare products. Tara wasn't sure she believed her, although she had no reason not to, but even as a girl Alice tended to play with the truth, alter the facts. She would make up stories in ways that served no purpose and lying for its own sake was often a sign of some deeper trauma. Tara had already moved to England by the time The Troubles in Northern Ireland started, but Alice was a teenager and had lived through the worst of it.

As Tara put her dishes in the sink, she looked out the kitchen window and saw a car in front of the cottage. The sight of it gave her a sudden panic until she remembered the new tenant was due to arrive, a fact she confirmed by glancing over at the calendar on the wall. An American, he had written to inquire about the house after seeing the ad her aunt had placed in a Boston newspaper. Tara spoke with him the summer before, a brief, staticky conversation from the payphone in the village to finalize the rental terms and set a date. Considering that there were plenty of Brits and French looking to rent, she thought it strange to advertise overseas, but her aunt insisted, "Americans complained a lot, but they always paid in cash."

Tara rushed to get ready so she could stop down and introduce herself before driving into the city. She walked into the bathroom, slipped out of her gown, and stepped into the tiny shower, her body covered in goosebumps. The pleasure of the hot water was no match for the chill in the air, however, and after quickly rubbing some soap all over, she got out and dried off. The moment she brought the towel to her face, she froze. Buried deep in the fibers of the towel was the smell of Kevin. It was too early to cry—she knew that if she started now, she would be emotional all day, and she had to be calm for her meeting with

Alice. But the grief was enough to affect her physically, and she staggered over to the sink, clutching it with both hands. She waited to get her balance and then looked up, staring into the fogged mirror. Her shoulders were hunched; her breasts sagged under the weight of middle age. Every day she did something to enhance her appearance, whether it was painting her nails, styling her hair, or shaving her legs. With all she had lost, she refused to let go of her femininity and, in some ways, she did it to honor him.

After a few minutes, Tara regained her composure and went into the bedroom. These spells never lasted long but their intensity made up for their brevity. As she opened the armoire and reached for a sweater, her towel fell to the floor, filling her with a mischievous delight. Back in London, she never would have stood naked with the window open, but on this lonely peninsula, she didn't care who saw her, and it was unlikely that someone would. Aside from the cottage, which she couldn't see from the bedroom, the next nearest neighbor was a quarter-mile away. She chuckled to herself in thinking that, of all the things she lost in coming out here, she had gained the freedom to dress in the nude.

She put on her jeans, stretching them over her hips, which seemed to be growing wider and more misshapen with each year. She couldn't deny that she was feeling old, and at thirty-seven, what woman wouldn't? She was still trim for her age, something she attributed to never having given birth, and she saw what childbearing did to her friends. But an intact figure wasn't worth not having a family, and since she was a little girl, she had always dreamed of becoming a mother.

Tara put on her boots and went over to the dresser, opening the top drawer and reaching for the leather wallet Kevin bought for her at Harrod's on their first anniversary. As she held it, she remembered how shiny it was that day, the smooth patent leather, the gleaming brass buttons. Now it was old, much like herself, its black stain faded at the corners, cracked along the seams like an aged horse saddle.

She slid her fingers into the semi-hidden pocket behind her driver's license and took out another identification card. Gazing down, she rubbed her thumb over the picture, the face of a woman much younger, bristling with the optimism of youth. She thought back to when it was taken, that day she stood nervously in a queue at the photo shop in East Belfast. In moments like this, it was hard to make the connection between that time and now. Before she put it away, her eyes swept the name on it, a name that seemed more foreign, more unfamiliar every time she saw it: Gwendolyn Marie Evers.

Three

JAMES'S EYES FLICKERED OPEN. IN THE HAZE OF THE morning light, it took him a moment to remember where he was, and he wasn't surprised because for the past few years he had moved around like a gypsy from one apartment to another. He sat up, his shoulders stiff from the narrow couch, and made his way over to the kitchen, where he rummaged through the cupboard looking for a glass but only finding teacups, all worn and chipped. He filled one under the faucet, drank it down, and had two more. The water was salty but he was parched, and his head pounded from dehydration.

James filled the old cast-iron kettle and lit the burner. As he waited for it to boil, he took his luggage into the bedroom, something he had intended to do the previous night before falling asleep on the couch. He dragged his duffle bag and suitcase down the hallway, turning into the first door. The moment he stepped inside, he felt a warm nostalgia in remembering the summers he slept here with his brother. The room was sparser now, with only a single bed, dresser, and a table in the corner. The walls were bare, cracked in places, and there were water stains on the ceiling. He wasn't sure if the home was more rundown, or if he just didn't notice such things as a child.

The floor creaked as he walked over to the window, and when he lifted the shade, he could see his cousins' old house about a football field away. The sun was high, close to noon he guessed, but he had forgotten to wind his watch so he wasn't sure.

When the kettle whistled, James grabbed the can of Folger's he brought from the States and ran out to turn it off. Because he had no coffee filters, he strained the grounds through a white napkin that he found in a drawer. He hadn't eaten since lunch the day before, but hunger didn't bother him, and if he had learned anything in the War, it was how to live with deprivation. He could always eat later, he told himself, and although there really was no rush, he was eager to get started on his work.

He took out the typewriter, its metal housing cold and damp, and placed it on the table by the couch. He had a sip of coffee, cupping the mug in both hands to stave off the morning chill. He set the margins, slid a piece of paper in, and turned the cylinder, locking it in place. Taking a deep breath, he pushed the carriage all the way over and began to type.

Dear Mr. Ledbetter,

I received your letter on December 4th regarding the lawsuit against my business associate Robert J. Dunford. I wholly dispute his accusation that the funds for our company, Dunford & Sons Construction, were in his power to administer...

Associate. It sounded hollow, almost deceptive, but considering it was the word his brother's attorney had used, James decided to respond in kind. Although he could feel his blood pressure rising, he no longer gave in to the anger, having resigned himself and his life to the facts of what happened.

· · ·

...At the time I left for the Marines, my father was the sole owner of the company. My brother and I had worked for him since high school with the understanding that we would both one day have a stake in the business. On several occasions, my father had stated his intention that, as the oldest son, I would become the company president while my brother would manage operations...

He had only finished a few sentences when the words began to fade. In the shadowy morning light, he couldn't tell if it was real or an illusion brought on by fatigue, stress, and his declining eyesight. He bought the ink just before leaving Boston and realized that it might have dried out on the flight. Nevertheless, he let out more ribbon and continued, pressing down harder as he went.

In the summer of '67, my father died suddenly. I was serving with a combat unit in Vietnam and my brother was temporarily acting as president of Dunford & Sons Construction. It was only when I returned home that I learned that my father had left no will...

The strikers smacked against the paper, the roller dinging at the end of each line. With his left hand maimed from shrapnel, James could no longer write, but he could type as fast as he could think. When his index finger slipped between the keys, he split a nail and yelled out loud. Frustrated, he got up to get more coffee when suddenly there was a noise. He stopped to listen, turning his ear and holding his breath, but all he heard was the drip of the leaky faucet, something he noted so he could fix it later.

As he started to walk, he heard the sound again and realized it was outside. He went over to the door, turned the rusted knob, and opened it.

"You again?"

Standing there was the dog, its hind legs down and peering up with longing eyes. James had the urge to slam the door but didn't because he knew it probably just wanted food. And considering his own hunger pangs, he felt a sympathy for the animal that he wouldn't normally have.

"Wait here," he said.

He went into the kitchen and opened the icebox, recoiling from the stench of an old milk carton and not much else. He looked in the cabinets but there was only a bag of flour, a couple of jars of spices. On the counter next to a ceramic jar he saw a tin, and when he looked inside, there were a few old biscuits, stale but not moldy. Animals would eat anything, he told himself, thinking back to how he and his friends once fed the carcass of a crow to a Dobermann.

James grabbed the biscuits, ran towards the door and when he opened it, he was surprised to see a woman. She was a few years younger, with dark eyes and dark hair, and she stood with a polite smile.

"You must be Mr. Dunford?" she said.

James looked past her and out to the yard.

"You see a dog?"

"Pardon?"

"A dog—a yellow dog. Looked like a stray."

"Every animal is a stray around here, the sheep, the cattle, the foxes. There's wild horses just on the other side of the hill."

"He was just here. I got him these."

James opened his hand to expose the biscuits, most of which had broken in his grasp.

"Rest assured, if he's hungry, he'll be back," she said.

Standing at the threshold, his body against the door, James stared out with a vague bewilderment. After a few seconds of awkward silence, she stepped forward and held out her hand.

"Tara Doherty," she said. "I live up at the main house. We spoke last summer on the phone."

James shifted the biscuits to his bad hand and shook with his good one, her soft, warm skin a pleasure to touch.

"Are you the landlord?"

"Hardly," she said with a laugh. "That would be my auntie. I'm just staying here...temporarily."

James forced a smile but didn't respond.

"So, have you found everything okay?"

He watched her eyes sweep the front of the cottage, from the weather-beaten walls to the old door, splintered and peeling.

"I know it's not much to look at," she went on as if to apologize. "But it'll hold up to the weather."

"Actually, I was thinking of cleaning it up a bit."

Tara raised her eyebrows.

"Suit yourself, Mr. Dunford. Don't feel obliged, of course. The price is reflective of the condition."

He acknowledged her with a quick nod and nothing more. When she cleared her throat, James took it as a sign that the conversation was over, and he was glad for it because he wasn't interested in talking with anyone.

"Okay, then," she said. "If you need anything, call up to the house."

She made a faint, almost disappointed smile and then turned to go. He stared as she walked away, captivated by her figure, slender but shapely, her hips swaying with each step. It was more out of curiosity than desire, however, because he hadn't spoken to a woman in months, and the mere sight of her was a mystery.

Tara stooped to get in the car, a beige two-door Opel Kadett that could have been an oversized golf cart. Suddenly, James remembered something and called to her, almost as an afterthought.

"Say, Miss?—"

"Tara," she said, glancing up.

"Tara. You wouldn't know where to get a typewriter ribbon?"

She tilted her head thinking, her dark hair blowing in the wind.

"What kind?"

"It's a Smith Corona."

She looked at him across the hood of the car.

"I'm going into Galway. I could try to get one."

"I'd appreciate it," he said.

"I'll do my best."

She nodded back with the same indifference he had shown her, the cheery pep gone from her face. If it was some kind of payback, James thought, he respected her all the more for it because he hated meekness.

She made a wide U-turn on the gravel and drove off, the small hatchback sputtering up the road and vanishing behind the hedgerows.

Once she was gone, the steady silence resumed, the only sound the waves, the breeze, the cry of cormorants somewhere offshore. James stood thinking about the woman far longer than expected, and he blamed it on the dreamy haze caused by jetlag.

As he turned to go back in, he could sense someone or something watching, and when he looked back, it was the dog.

"You're a regular pest."

It came closer, its tail wagging, cautiously excited.

"You made me look like a fool, boy. I told her you were out here."

When the animal barked, James took it as an apology, and he accepted. He tossed the biscuits on the ground, and it ran over and devoured them up like it hadn't seen food in weeks. Wiping his hands, James watched it eat and something about the dog's manner was familiar, the way it raised its lips before biting or the slurping sound it made. For some reason, he thought of Joel Rodriguez, his nineteen-year-old platoon sergeant from Del Rio, Texas. Whenever they went out on patrol, he brought beef jerky, and he chomped so loudly that the men joked he would give away their position.

James chuckled to himself and rubbed his chin, overcome by that mix of nostalgia and grief which came from thinking about friends who were gone. He was startled when the dog looked up and their eyes met. It abandoned its biscuit and came over, its head down and whimpering, and James knelt to pet it. Its fur was knotted, and its skin was covered in small bumps from ticks, mites, and fleas. As James ran his hands along the animal's side, he could feel its ribs protruding, some of them cracked or misshapen, the brutality of life in the wild. Maybe it had been kicked by a horse, he thought, or trampled by a herd of sheep. He shook his head, sighed, and pulled the dog closer. James wasn't much for the company of people or pets, but he knew what it was like to be worn down by life.

"What's this world done to you, boy?"

Four

〜

THE N59 WAS A TWO-LANE ROADWAY THAT RAN THROUGH the heart of Connemara, skirting the mountains and connecting the few scattered villages along the fifty-mile stretch between Clifden and Galway. For the past two hours, Tara had driven with both hands tight around the wheel while cars and trucks zoomed past, at some points only inches from her door. She hated driving in Ireland—she hated to drive anywhere. Her years in London without an automobile had freed her from the manic frenzy of streets and highways. Out here the roads were treacherous, carved from carriage paths and lined with tall hedgerows. Every time a vehicle approached from the opposite direction, it seemed like it was coming straight at her, a sensation that left her constantly on edge.

As Tara came into the city, the streets were bustling in the noonday rush, people flocking to pubs and restaurants for lunch. A few foreigners were obvious among the crowds, Germans and French mostly, but the tourist shops were closed for the winter. Seeing the taillights of a lorry, Tara pulled over and waited for it to leave before backing into the spot. Then she turned off the engine and sat quietly, her hands clammy and heart racing. She had always been anxious, something she attributed to growing up in Belfast, but now whenever she came into a city—any city—she experienced a full-on panic.

It started to drizzle. Looking at her watch, she realized it was time to go so she grabbed her purse and reached under the seat for her umbrella. She opened the door and stepped out onto the narrow sidewalk, where people turned to get by her. She walked quickly, her head down to avoid making eye contact, and when she reached the next corner, she saw the sign for The Raven, a small pub nestled between an Indian restaurant and a betting parlor.

Just as she went to cross, someone called her name and she froze. Glancing back, she was relieved to see her sister coming through the crowd with a big grin. Alice had on a beaded coat and waist-high jeans that were faded and flared at the bottom. She looked like a hippie ten years too late but parts of Ireland were always behind in fashion.

"Did I scare ya?" she asked.

"You startled me."

"Isn't that the same thing?"

Tara gave a sour smile and they hugged, more as a formality than as a genuine show of emotion. She loved her sister, but they had spent so much of their lives apart that sometimes she felt like she didn't really know her.

"Your voice sounded different," Tara said.

"I've had a terrible cold."

Tara looked away with a skeptical smirk and they stepped into the street. She could smell the marijuana on Alice, see the glassy-eyed daze of intoxication. She had always been more strait-laced than her sister, never dabbling in drugs or risky sex, even at the height of Sixties hedonism. Tara couldn't blame Alice for rebelling, however, and she probably would have too if she had stayed in Belfast. The generation that lived through the riots and rock-throwing needed some way to escape.

They crossed over and walked into The Raven, a dank, dark pub that was more of a local establishment than a place for tourists or professionals. The ceiling was low, the floors wide-plank, and the walls were covered with pictures of Galway teams, hurling and Irish football. They sat at a table by the window and took off their coats, which were damp from the rain.

"This weather," Tara said with a sigh.

"The sun was out in Fermanagh."

"How was the drive down?"

"The border was awful, soldiers damn near tore my backseat out. Walter wanted me to go through Enniskillen, but it would've added an hour. How're things out in the boondocks?"

"Deadly quiet, as usual."

"Not necessarily a bad thing."

A young waitress came over, dressed like a punk rocker with Dr. Martens boots, black jeans, and spiked hair.

"Afternoon, ladies. What can I get ye?"

"I'll have a pint of Guinness," Alice said, then looked at Tara.

"Um, just tea, please."

The woman left, and they sat facing each other with hesitant smiles.

"So," Alice began. "Auntie says there's a tenant."

"An American."

"Is he handsome?"

Tara rolled her eyes, almost embarrassed by the question, and she tried to think of some way to describe James.

"He's...quiet," she said.

"Who on earth would move out there in winter?—"

They were interrupted by the waitress, who put down the drinks, a couple of napkins, and then walked away. Alice took a sip, the pint glass giant in her waifish hand. She wiped the foam from her lips and reached into her bag for an envelope.

"Da had some things from the old house he wanted you to have."

She opened it and pulled out a stack of photos, color and black & white. On top was a picture of their mother, who had been dead now for over ten years. It was taken at an angle, like all portrait photos, and just enough to hide the mole on the left side of her chin. Her face was smooth, her hair in a tall bun. She was somewhere in her mid-twenties, Tara thought, and was probably dating their father at the time. It couldn't have been a graduation photo because their mother never went to college so it must have been for her job at Ulster Hospital, or maybe a church group.

"So beautiful," Tara said.

"Isn't she? There are lots more. You'll go through them later."

"How is Da?"

"Gettin' on okay," Alice said, taking another sip. "He worries about you."

Tara's face strained and she looked away. As selfish as it was, she didn't want to know how he felt because it would only make her feel guilty.

"When do you think I can visit?" Tara asked.

"Walter says the trial will probably start next month."

"Couldn't I come up for just a day?"

"I don't know," Alice said with a cringing expression. "Things are pretty tense up north. I know you're removed from it all...living out here."

As she said it, they heard grumbling and looked to see some men gathered at the end of the bar, pints in hand and staring at a television. The news was on, and images of British Prime Minister Margaret Thatcher and Northern Ireland MP Bernadette Devlin flashed across the screen. IRA inmates were renewing their struggle to be recognized as political prisoners rather than criminals, threatening another hunger strike if their demands weren't met.

Once the segment ended, they turned back to each other.

"I'm not as removed as you'd think," Tara said.

"I didn't mean it like that."

Tara pursed her lips, taking it as an apology and wishing she hadn't been so curt. As she sipped her tea, she noticed a gold cross around Alice's neck, and it offered a good opportunity to change the subject.

"That's lovely," she said.

Her sister looked down, touched the pendant.

"Thanks. Walter got it for me."

"A sort of pre-engagement?"

"Oh my," Alice said with a sarcastic flair. "Who knows?"

Tara had first met Walter when he came to her parents' house for dinner a week after Kevin's funeral. He was a typical guy from East Belfast, sports-crazed and sturdily built, and he worked as an apprentice riveter in the shipyards. Tara only saw him a few times after that, mainly because she lived abroad. But he had shown enough concern for her safety after the death of Kevin that she felt like she knew him and would have happily had him for a brother-in-law. No one in her sister's generation seemed interested in marriage, however, and considering all the stress and uncertainty of living in a war zone, Tara understood why.

"Don't let the years get ahead of you," Tara said.

It was feeble advice and she knew it, but she intended it more for herself than for her sister.

The conversation moved on to trivial things, the cost of petrol, Alice's job at the hair salon, the latest Elvis Costello album. Tara smiled as she listened, but with seven years between them, she could never really connect with her sister much beyond serious matters. And she was glad when Alice finished her pint and looked around because it meant that she, too, was ready to go.

"Shall we be off?"

"Let's," Tara said.

"Sorry, I can't stay longer."

"Thanks for driving down."

"Not at all," Alice said. "It's always nice to get away from...all that."

They got the bill from the waitress, and when Alice tried to pay, Tara wouldn't let her. As they walked past the bar, everyone turned, and Tara was quite content to know they were gawking at her sister. She no longer craved the lurid attention of men, or at least she told herself that.

They left the pub, and the rain had stopped, leaving a sheen of dull gray over the entire City. Water dripped from awnings and overhangs, and many people still had their umbrellas open, anticipating the next downpour.

They walked to the corner and stopped, facing each other with the poignant awkwardness of any farewell.

"I'll write soon," Alice said.

"Please do."

"Walter says if you need anything, let us know."

"I will."

"This will all pass soon enough, love."

"I know."

When they hugged, Tara could smell beer and cigarettes on her breath, and it reminded her of home. Growing up, it was a common combination, mostly among men but women too, the elixir for the working-class doldrums. Tara never smoked and she only drank wine, a fact that, in times like this, made her feel something of a snob.

"By for now," Alice whispered.

Just as they let go, it began to sprinkle. Alice stepped back, blew a kiss, and then turned around and was gone. Tara opened her umbrella and went in the opposite direction, momentarily lost until she recognized an electronics shop that she passed by earlier. As she walked, her eyes began to well up, and even if people noticed, it was always easier to cry in the rain. She continued for another block with her head down, and by the time she reached the car, she had regained her composure.

As she opened the door, her eyes swept a stationary shop across the road, and she remembered the typewriter ribbon for James. She darted across and went inside, where a man with thinning dark hair and glasses looked up from behind the counter.

"May I help you?" he said.

"Typewriter ribbon, please," she said.

"What sort, Miss?"

Tara struggled to remember, still distracted from her meeting with Alice.

"Smith Corona!" she exclaimed.

"Model?"

"Not sure. It's a portable."

"Color?"

"Black."

The attendant nodded and looked through the boxes of ribbons on the shelf behind him.

"Any half-inch ribbon should do," he said, turning around. "Just one?"

"For now," she said with a polite smile.

As she handed him the money, he squinted, staring at her with a strange concentration.

"Gwen?" he said.

"Pardon?"

"Gwen Evers?"

In those two short words, she heard the accent that she had grown up around, and it sent a shudder through her body.

"It's Mal Davies," he said, "from Campbell Secondary—"

Tara got a sudden hot flash—she had the urge to drop everything and run. But she calmly took the change and the ribbon, muttering under her breath as she turned to leave, "I'm sorry, I believe you're mistaken."

Five

James sat on the couch, the crumbs of his toast on a plate beside him along with grease from the fatty bacon he had fried. The cabinets were stocked with crackers, bread, a bag of potatoes, many still covered in dirt. The icebox had a quart of fresh milk, some lamb chops wrapped in paper, a block of salted butter. He had found the nearest village after driving two miles down the coast road, and it was little more than a collection of adjoined farmhouses. But he was able to get everything he needed, including WD-40, which his father taught him could be used to revive old typewriter ribbon.

James sprayed some on a rag and wiped it gently along the tape, enough to moisturize the ink without removing it. He closed the top and slid the carriage over, ready to begin a new line on the letter he had started the previous day.

As he began to type, the words appeared in dark, vibrant letters, and he knew the oil had worked. The fingernail he broke was still split, the dried blood coalesced around the cuticle, so he proceeded carefully because he had no whiteout and didn't want to make a mistake.

. . .

...I will withdraw my lawsuit against Robert J. Dunford under the condition that any stake or equity I may be entitled to be liquidated and that the money be given to Alva Dunford, 76 Bayfield Road, Quincy, Massachusetts. If the defendant does not consent to these terms, I will proceed with the lawsuit and seek full damages for being denied my rightful ownership in Dunford & Sons Construction...

James stared at the page, wavering between feelings of cowardice and triumph. The litigation against his brother had dragged on for too long, and sometimes being a good soldier meant knowing when to retreat. He wasn't giving up, he told himself, but finally letting go of something that had consumed his life like a cancer. His ex-wife had borne the brunt of it, and after her years of quietly tolerating his anger and outbursts, she deserved some small compensation for her troubles. Still, it was the hardest noble thing he had ever done.

He got up to stretch and get more coffee. As he walked by the door, he opened it and looked out.

"Still thirsty, Rod?"

Lying against the house, the dog looked up, his ears twitching. Already he recognized the name James had given him when he stepped out that morning to find the animal sleeping on the doorstep. In Rod, James saw an eerie resemblance to his platoon sergeant, although he couldn't explain how or why. But he was moved enough to feel in some way responsible, and he even bought a bag of dry food, put out a blanket and fresh water.

James reached down for the bowl and Rod whimpered. He filled it under the tap, put it back outside, and then got more coffee. He sat down on the couch, and the moment he resumed typing the words began to fade. Taking out the ribbon, he dabbed on more WD-40 and tried again but it only left a damp smudge, ruining the letter he would now have to rewrite.

He shook his head, the anger rising within him like a spasm.

"Goddammit!"

In an instant, he picked up the typewriter and hurled it across the room, where it bounced off the wall and landed on the floor in a cloud of plaster dust. He stood fuming and out of breath, fists clenched and trembling all over.

Suddenly, there was a tap at the door.

He turned, as if coming out of a spell, and felt embarrassed. He went over and opened it to see Tara.

"Everything okay?"

"Yeah," he said. "Just, um, knocked over a pot."

She had on a long coat and pink sweater, her lipstick as dark as her eyes, and just her presence seemed to calm him, something he hadn't experienced from a woman in years.

"I got you this."

James cringed when he saw the typewriter ribbon—a few seconds too late.

"Thank you."

"I see you've found him?" she said, glancing over at Rod.

Excited by the attention, the dog got up and came over with his tail wagging.

"More like he found me."

"You'll discover that friends can be hard to come by out here," Tara said, crouching to pet him. She ran her hands through his knotted hair, down his back, under the scruff of his neck. "Just riddled with tics, poor thing. And so thin."

"I bought him some food this morning."

"So, you found the village."

"You call that a village?"

"Not by American standards, of course. Amazing what one shop can keep though, isn't it?"

James nodded and she stood back up, Rod lingering at her side, hoping for more affection.

"Well," she said. "I'll be on my way."

She walked over to her car, its tires and fenders caked with mud.

"Any idea whose dog this is?" James said.

"Like you said, Mr. Dunford—"

"James—"

"*James,*" she said, acknowledging the courtesy. "Most likely a stray."

"It's a wonder he survives."

"It's a wonder any of us do."

With that, Tara got in and started the engine. She gave a quick wave, and James watched as she turned around and drove off, leaving him to wonder what she meant.

~

James sat hunched over the typewriter with a butter knife, unbending the bars that were damaged by the impact. The machine was spared, but there was a deep gouge on the wall, exposing portions of the old wooden beam that held it together. Once the parts were back in place, he tapped a few keys and they worked.

Still, James was ashamed of losing his temper, knowing that fixing something didn't always make up for the fact that you broke it. The spells of violent rage came on like a seizure, taking over his entire body and forcing him to do things he always regretted. He wanted to blame it on the war, a nervous system gone haywire from the stress and trauma, but the truth was, he was angry long before Vietnam.

He installed the new ribbon and put in a blank piece of paper. He took a last drag on his cigarette and stamped it out on the tea saucer he used for an ashtray, now covered with dozens of misshapen butts, the accumulation of days. James could speak well enough to navigate life, but he wasn't clever with words, and he had been thinking for months about what he would say.

Dear Alva,

I got your address from your sister and I hope you don't mind that I've written. I am currently in Ireland, renting the small cottage where my grandmother used to live. I know we always talked about coming here and I am disappointed we never made it because it's beautiful.

For a long time, I was afraid to call or write because of how I treated you. But I've reached a point in my life where I want to make right as many of the wrongs as I can. I've been thinking a lot about my past, not just the situation with my brother but also the war. I was just a kid when I went in and never realized how it would affect me...

James heard a faint tapping, and when he looked over, icy flakes were smacking against the window. It seldom snowed in Ireland, but the harsh mix of wind, rain, and cold did a good impression of it. With the temperature close to freezing, the turf fire struggled to keep up, and there was a chill in the air. James rubbed his hands together, lit another cigarette, and continued on.

I never blamed you because we couldn't have children. If anything I blame myself for wanting to bring kids into our lives when I wasn't prepared for it. I know that you tried and I'm sorry...

He stopped again, distracted by something but not sure what. He got up and walked towards the kitchen, maybe to make more coffee or get some water—he really didn't know. As he passed the front door, he remembered something and reached for the knob. Leaning out into the rain, he looked along the front of the house and saw Rod, curled up against the wall, his water and food bowls beside him.

"Hey boy," he said.

The animal lifted his head, wagged his tail feebly. He struggled to rise, his legs unsteady, and James was tempted to help him. But Rod got up on his own and came over, his mangled ear visible in the dim light. Joel Rodriquez had a similar disfigurement, James thought, although he couldn't remember which side, and it was another bizarre coincidence.

The dog stopped at the threshold as if waiting for permission, and James waved him in.

"Don't you have anywhere to go?"

His hair soaked and paws dirty, Rod whimpered and waddled inside.

"That makes two of us."

Six

As Tara drove along the coast, grass and other debris flew across the road, kicked up from the Atlantic winds. The barbed wire fences which separated grazing plots rattled from the gusts, and the sheep that covered the hillside seemed to shiver in their coats. The sky was flat gray from the mountains to the horizon, the ocean a vast stretch of white-capped tumult. To a visitor from another place, it might have felt like a calm before the storm but on the distant shores of Connemara, it was just winter.

Tara often wondered what brought people out to this bleak land, whether its original inhabitants had chosen it for its remote beauty or whether they had been driven out here as punishment for some awful crime. In such a harsh and unforgiving place, the scenarios were as extreme as the climate.

She wondered, too, why James had come out here to live. As her only neighbor within earshot, she thought about him often, his unkempt hair and scruff, his low voice and one-word replies. He always answered the door in his socks and wearing the same clothes, faded denim jeans and a frayed flannel shirt. They had probably spoken less than ten minutes in total, and yet she could tell he was troubled. He could never quite look her in the eye, and he showed an intentional unfriendliness which she found to be insincere. Growing up in Belfast, with all its violence and bitterness, Tara had learned young how to spot a callous person, and she was sure that James was not one.

Aside from her observations about his character, she also couldn't deny that he was handsome. James was tall like her father, although not as broad, and he had the sturdy hands of a man who spent at least part of his life doing manual labor. Tara guessed he was slightly older than her—forty at the most—and if there was anything unfair about life, it was that men seemed to age better. Even so, his sideburns had grays, his eyes had wrinkles, and like anyone approaching midlife, he was beginning to show signs of wear. But Tara was no longer interested in physical characteristics—if she ever had been—and even as a girl, her sister Alice was more into good looks.

Soon the open fields of the coastal stretch gave way to a more thickly settled area, a suburb of sorts, and the road ascended gradually, winding through a tunnel of tall hedgerows that blocked out the view. Tara passed a stone church and slowed down as she came into a village, a cluster of one-story buildings that were originally homes. At the corner was a gas station, followed by a row of small businesses—a hardware store, hostel, and a tourist shop that was only open during summer. The center of town was Joyce's, a combination pub, post office, and market which sold everything from steaks to staples.

Tara parked in front and got out, smiling at an old woman with a cane. She always worried what people thought of her out here—did they see her as just another blow-in or worse, did they recognize her? Locals were never unwelcoming, but a long history of exploitation by Protestant landlords and other outsiders gave them a certain quiet suspicion. And although Tara understood, it made her feel more exposed, and she preferred the anonymity of the city.

When she walked into Joyce's, there was a group of workers at the bar, dressed in smocks and rubber boots, empty dinner plates in front of them. Behind the counter, Jerry the owner was pouring a pint, his white hair combed back, a towel around his neck. Seeing Tara, he held up his finger, and she walked over to the shop side and waited.

In the far corner, the television was on and it was more of the same: images of the Maze prison, gaunt IRA prisoners dressed in blankets,

British soldiers standing with rifles and flak jackets on street corners in Belfast. Even though she turned away, the sight of it gave her a sickening feeling, and she was relieved when Jerry came over.

"Now Miss," he said. "What can I get ye?"

She had been coming into Joyce's since she arrived the summer before, and although she knew his name, he still didn't know hers and she liked it that way.

"A half a side of ham, a quart of milk. Have you any peas?"

"Just what's on the shelf over there," he said.

He walked out back to the storeroom, and she went over to the dry goods, two rows of wooden shelves that wouldn't have accounted for an endcap in a London market. She got a box of Barry's Tea, some biscuits, dishwashing soap, and a bag of dried peas, the last one in stock.

Jerry came back out with the ham and milk, and Tara met him at the register. Nothing was marked, but he seemed to know the price of everything. He rang in the items, one at a time, conducting himself with a soft and steady dignity.

When Tara was a girl, her family owned a candy store—the fantasy of every child—and she and her sister would go there every day after school. Her father always insisted he needed their help, but they never did much work, and she realized as she got older that it was mostly to watch them while their mother worked at the laundromat. In the summer of her last year in college, the shop was destroyed by fire in the riots and he never reopened, instead getting a job as a mechanic at his cousin's garage in Lisburn. She would never forget the magical smells, the licorice and toffee, Ritchie's Milky Mints and Cadbury chocolate bars.

"Miss?"

Tara looked up, embarrassed that she had spaced out.

"Pardon?" she said.

"I said, *you've a new neighbor?*"

"Word certainly gets around."

"He was in just yesterday morning," Jerry said. "Odd to see a Yank this time of year."

"I just hope he left enough food for the rest of us."

He raised his eyebrows, acknowledging the insinuation as Americans were known for buying all they could.

"Seemed more interested in paint. Bought five gallons of it. Brushes, nails, and sandpaper too."

Tara winced at the news but otherwise didn't know how to respond. Jerry pressed a button, the drawer sprung open, and he looked up. "Four pounds twenty, please."

She paid him, and he put everything in a paper bag and handed it to her.

"Thanks, Jerry."

"Oh," he said as she turned to go. "He left his change. Would you mind taking it to him?"

He reached under the counter and handed her an envelope.

"Not at all," she said.

Tara went slowly along the coast road, trying to extend the drive back because, aside from a short walk before dinner, it was the most she would do all day. Her life felt like a long purgatory, the weeks and months passing by in a haze of repetition that left her sometimes forgetting the date. The only thing that kept her sane was knowing that, at some point, she would be able to leave, returning to London or even back to Belfast. It wasn't that she didn't love Connemara, but no place felt permanent without the love of family and friends around.

She pulled up to the house and parked, getting the bag from the backseat and bringing it inside. As she put away the groceries, she checked to see if there was pepper for the split pea soup. Considering there would be enough food for several people, she thought of inviting James for dinner then decided it might be too forward because he had only recently arrived. She had no intention of disturbing him, but as the only two people on this narrow spit of land, it would be strange not to interact eventually.

She washed her hands and went into the refrigerator for the carrots and onions. As she chopped them, she glanced out the kitchen window to the cottage. James was a mystery, arriving alone in the dead of winter, and she couldn't help but wonder why. Maybe he came to recover from some tragic life event, a death or a divorce, she thought, or he was running from the law. Her mother used to say she was nosy, but Tara's interest in other people was never for gossip, and she only ever wanted to know their story.

Tara diced up some ham, put it in a pot with the vegetables and milk, thyme and a bay leaf. Leaving it to simmer, she got her coat and umbrella and headed out to give James his change from Joyce's. She walked across the yard, her boots squishing in the mud, and onto the road, stepping around wet rocks and avoiding puddles. The sky was overcast, the air damp. In seconds, her face was covered with a salty mist, but she didn't wipe it off, knowing it was good for the complexion.

When she reached the end, she turned into the yard and stopped. Gazing across, she was amazed by how different the cottage looked. The door had new black paint; the trim around the windows had been touched up. The overgrown weeds and grass which once covered the property had been cut and put into piles. The small improvements were a big transformation, and it warmed her heart to see them. Her aunt never meant to let the home fall into disrepair and was always embarrassed by it. But as an old woman on a pension, she didn't have the money to restore it and had even considered tearing it down.

"Hello."

Tara spun around, gasping.

"Sorry, did I scare you?"

Standing behind her was James, dressed in a heavy wool coat and hat, a shovel in hand.

"It doesn't take much, I'm afraid," she said.

"Can I help you?"

She held out the envelope and he stared at it.

"Your change," she explained. "From Joyce's. You forgot it."

"Keep it. I owe you for the ink."

"Thank you," she said, then she looked over at the house. "It's wonderful, what you've done. Auntie will be thrilled."

James simply nodded, leaning on the shovel and looking at her with a quiet intensity that almost made her blush.

"So, you're handy?" she said.

"My father was a builder."

She waited to see if he would elaborate and wasn't surprised when he didn't. She could have pressed the conversation, but she already felt like she was intruding and, with the soup cooking on the stove, it seemed an appropriate time to go.

"Well, I'm sorry to bother you—"

"No bother," he interrupted.

When their eyes met, she smiled shyly and started to walk away.

"Tara," he said, and she stopped. As she turned around, she realized it was the first time he'd ever spoken her name. "Do you know where I can mail some letters?"

"Joyce's would be the closest," she said.

"They do mail too?"

Tara stood thinking, probably longer than she needed to.

"You'll find that out here people have to offer everything they can."

Seven

JAMES CHARGED ACROSS THE BLUFF, SQUINTING IN THE stark light of the late afternoon sun. The rain that morning left everything damp, and his boots sank in the soft, mossy ground. To the north, the hills of Mayo rose majestically on the far side of Killary Fjord, their valleys darkened by the shadows of the clouds. To the south, the coast went for miles unending in a patchwork of pastures, peat bogs, and stone walls.

He soon came down to the water, where the jagged shore of headlands and rocky inlets gave way to a beach. As he walked along the sand, he looked towards the islands and recalled the time his uncle took him and his brother out in a small skiff. A sudden change in weather that day had turned the waves to small mountains, and by the time they got back, they were seasick and soaked to the bone. The only reason his mother didn't throw a fit was because they weren't her relatives, but for the rest of the trip, she wouldn't let her children leave her side.

His mother never loved Ireland as much as his father did, and James wasn't ever sure she liked it. She complained about everything from the weather to the high cost of milk, and even on nice days, she would be fixed to the Bakelite radio, listening to some RTE drama she could barely understand. As a woman whose own Gaelic forbears had come to America three generations before, she had none of the romantic nostalgia of her husband, and about the only thing they agreed on was that Connemara was a safe place for kids to spend a summer.

James heard voices and saw three boys up ahead. As he got closer, they all looked towards the bluff and Rod burst onto the sand, leaping in the air like a bronco. When he didn't show up the night before, James started to worry, and he had never been more relieved to see a mangy stray.

"Hey," he called out, and they turned around.

Hearing his voice, Rod ran straight over, circling him in a frenzy of excitement until James patted him and he calmed down.

"Any idea whose dog this is?" James said.

The boys stood still, arms at their sides, dressed in oversize coats which he could tell were hand-me-downs.

"I've never seen him, sir," the tallest one replied.

"How 'bout you?" James said to the other two.

They shook their heads.

"Where do you all live?"

"Just beyond," the middle one said, pointing towards the shallow hill on the north side of the peninsula.

"How'd you like to make a few bucks?" he asked, and they all looked confused. "American dollars. Wanna make some money?"

Instantly, they all smiled and nodded.

"I'm staying at the cottage over there. Come by tomorrow after school."

"Yes, thank you, sir."

James walked away and Rod followed, his tongue out and panting from all the exercise.

"What's got into you, boy?"

He reached down and stroked the dog's neck, running his fingers through the knotted hair. He had only fed Rod a few times, and already he was gaining weight. And his energy was back too because the moment James let him go, he shot forward and ran off. Not to be outdone by a dog, James went after him, but his boots were no match for the swiftness of paws, and soon Rod was at the top of the bluff. By the time James got there, the animal was halfway across an open field, panicking a flock of sheep before leaping over a stone wall.

James struggled to close the gap, dodging clumps of grass, his feet getting bogged down in the marshy soil. At times, the dog's yellow coat blended in so well with the dry vegetation that James couldn't see him. Nevertheless, he continued on, calling out and listening for Rod's bark. He went around a wall, walked across a pasture, and stepped over a barbed-wire fence. Caught in a small glade, he was momentarily lost until he came out to a clearing with a house.

As he slowed down to catch his breath, he noticed movement in a window and looked closer to see the silhouette of a naked woman. He stopped midstep, stunned by the image, staring at her pale white skin, her full but sagging breasts. After his divorce, James had lost all desire for sex or love or female company, and now he found himself as spellbound as a hormonal teen. In those few seconds, some part of him was awoken that had been dormant for a long time.

As he turned to go, he heard rustling, and Rod came out of the bushes. James looked over with a silent dread, finger to his lips as if the dog would know what he meant.

"Arf!"

The moment he barked, James cringed. He glanced over to the window and was further horrified when the woman looked out. It was Tara. Whether she shut the curtains or just covered up, he would never know because he instantly turned away and ducked behind the trees. He went down a small slope, Rod close on his heels, and they came out to the road, only a dozen or so yards from the cottage. As they walked, the dog tried to get his attention, but James ignored him until they got to the yard.

"You just embarrassed the shit outta me, you know that?"

Rod tilted his head in confusion, then reared up and down, let out a sharp yelp. James was still mad, but he knew he couldn't blame an animal for having no tact. As he stared down at the dog, its mangled ear and scarred nose, he was again struck by the likeness of Sergeant Rodriguez, and it sent a chill through his body. Maybe it was the shape of his jawline, James thought, or the distance between his eyes. Whatever it was, it was real enough that he got unexpectedly choked up.

He shook his head, looked at Rod, and then gazed out, grounding himself in the immutability of the landscape.

"I must be losing my mind."

Eight

TARA SLEPT IN THE NUDE THAT NIGHT, CLINGING TO A PILE of down comforters, the sheets damp with the sweat of her anxiety. Some days she felt like she was going crazy, while on others she thought she was too sane. If she wasn't speaking to Kevin in her dreams, she was talking to him out loud, usually in the bed and sometimes in the shower, recounting her day or asking his advice about some trivial thing. Once he made her promise that, should anything happen to either one of them, they would go on living. But she was sure that, even in the throes of romantic pledges, exhibitionism wasn't what he had in mind.

Tara felt guilty and it wasn't just because James had seen her ass. Something about the encounter, as awkward as it was, made her feel wanted again, and she saw that as betrayal. She knew Kevin wouldn't object and probably would have laughed, but she was more troubled by her own reaction, the cheap arousal of an indiscreet moment. Every woman reached an age where being seen in the nude went from being an outrage to a thrill.

She didn't blame James because she knew he wasn't the peeping type. He probably went out for a walk, got lost, and was just as horrified as her when he stumbled onto her property. One of the paradoxes of such vast and open land was that it could be deceivingly disorienting.

When she first moved here, she went out to explore and, not paying attention, found herself caught in a maze of stonewalls, wire fences, and hedgerows, all the while her house plainly in sight.

Beyond her own concerns, Tara worried what James would think. The longer it went, the more uncomfortable they each would be, and the only proper thing to do was to go over and apologize.

As she came down the road, she heard voices, and when she turned into the yard, she was surprised to see three boys, dressed in the navy uniforms of the local national school. The oldest was cutting back more weeds with a scythe while the other two hauled away the refuse, putting it in piles. The stray dog was there too, scuttling between them like he was overseeing the project. He looked healthier than before, Tara thought, his coat shiny and his body less gaunt. She hated to see any animal suffer and was still traumatized from a trip with Kevin to Morocco, where hordes of wild cats, flea-ridden and half-starved, roamed the streets and marketplaces.

She looked around for James, but it wasn't until she saw a wooden ladder that she realized he was on the roof. He was crouched beside the chimney with his back to her, his boots braced against the slate shingles, one arm inside the flue. Not wanting to startle him, she walked quietly towards the house and looked up, hands on her hips and squinting.

"Is the view lovely?"

James stopped and glanced back, his hairline damp, his face strained from exertion. He paused to catch his breath then mumbled something she couldn't hear.

"Pardon, Mr. Dunford?" Tara said.

She didn't know why she used his surname and maybe it was nerves. But it was impossible to go back to cordial formalities with someone who had seen you buck naked.

With a grunt, James pulled his arm out of the chimney, and with it came a clump of dried twigs and leaves, blackened with soot. He tossed it over the edge, and it landed in a cloud of dust and ash.

"Bird's nest," he said, wiping his forehead.

She watched as he walked along the ridge of the roof, one foot on either side, and descended the ladder. The dog rushed over, and James patted the top of its head, ran his hand along its back. As he approached her, Tara saw that he had on a military jacket, and its olive-green made her uneasy. In her last year of college, the British Army was deployed to Belfast to stop sectarian rioting. Many residents were relieved, Catholics and Protestants alike, and she recalled her mother making little packets of chocolates and tarts which she handed out to the soldiers as they passed by the shop. The honeymoon didn't last, however, and soon both communities saw them as aggressors. A week after Tara left for London, the boy across the street was hit and killed by an armored military vehicle. Unlike her sister Alice, Tara wasn't around for the worst of the conflict, but the sight of combat fatigues still brought out feelings of sadness, fear, and resentment.

"Afternoon," James said, streaks of black on his forehead and cheeks.

"Good afternoon."

She managed a sour smile and squirmed, realizing then that maybe it was only she who was embarrassed by the incident.

"So, you are in the military?"

"Was," he said flatly.

"The American Army?"

"Marines."

The conversation was sparse as usual, with long and uncomfortable pauses between her questions and his short answers. She looked around the property, impressed by all the improvements, and if there was anything that could stimulate dialogue, it was asking someone about something they cared about.

"What you've done is amazing," she said. "What's left?"

"The garden."

"A garden?"

"My grandmother's," he said, pointing. "See the rows?"

When Tara looked over, all she saw was overgrown grass, bushes, shrubs, and the crumbling remains of an old stone wall. She didn't know if there was really a garden under it all, but she understood how the power of memories could make lost things seem only hidden.

"Well," she said. "You'd better wait 'til spring."

"As long as it takes—"

"Sir?"

They turned and the boys were coming towards them, hats askew and covered in dirt. Tara watched with a warm sympathy, knowing they probably had to wear the same clothes again tomorrow.

"We've gotta be home," one of the boys said.

James reached in his pants pocket, took out an old leather wallet.

"You want Irish or U.S.?" he said, a hint of mischief in his tone.

They looked sheepishly at one another, conferring with shrugs and silent glances. Finally, the oldest boy stepped forward and said, "U.S., Sir, please."

James took out some singles, darkened and frayed, and Tara wondered why American money was always so worn out. The boys held out their hands, palms up as if ready to receive communion, and their faces beamed when, one by one, James dispensed a few dollar bills.

"Now, be back tomorrow. Same time."

"Yes, sir," they responded in unison. "Thank you, sir."

As they walked off, Tara watched James watch them, his gaze intense, and she searched for signs of what he was thinking. Did they remind him of his childhood? Or did they make him think about his own children who were now, perhaps, all grown up?

"Are kids always so polite around here?" he asked, reaching in his coat for a cigarette.

"Weren't you at that age?"

As he lit it, he glanced up with an ironic smirk, then was suddenly distracted.

"Hey! Get the hell away from that!"

Tara looked and the dog had its nose in the bird's nest, shaking it side to side. When James ran over, she followed after him and said, "Listen, I wanted to apologize for the other day—"

Rod quickly fled and James stopped and turned to her.

"How do you mean?"

"When you came into my yard," she said.

"Your yard?"

"I saw you...from the window."

"Tara," he said, and she liked it when he said her name. "I can't see twenty feet in front of me."

Again, he walked off—he always seemed to be moving away from her—and she smiled to herself. She didn't know if he was being honest or just polite, but she was satisfied that the issue was settled.

James went over to the ladder, took it with both hands, and pulled it away from the side of the house. With the cigarette between his teeth, he slowly lowered the top half until it collapsed.

"Where'd you find that?"

"Those boys brought it," he said, laying it flat down against the side of the cottage.

"And where'd you find them?"

He ignored her question and said, "Any idea where I can get rid of all this brush?"

"Most people around here burn it."

"Burn it?" he said, and he flicked his cigarette. "Seems dangerous."

Tara watched as it landed on the ground, hissing in the wet grass, and she looked at him with a cute frown. He never said much, but she liked his humor, and sometimes sarcasm was its own form of communication.

The dog rushed back into the yard, its paws covered in mud and mouth open like it had a story to tell. It ran up to James and was just ready to jump when he held out his arms.

"Whoa, Rod," he said.

Tara smiled in surprise, looking first at the dog and then to James.

"Rod? You've named him?" she asked.

"Everything needs a name."

Nine

JAMES SAT TYPING IN THE KITCHEN ON THE WOBBLY TABLE he brought in from one of the bedrooms. He couldn't remember much about his grandmother's decor and assumed it had all been replaced by later owners. Yet there was something familiar about the piece, its hand-turned legs and uneven edges, and he wondered if it could have been hers, a holdover from the past. As he ran his hand along the top, he examined the dark patina and could see, covered under a newer coat of wax, the nicks and scratches of old wear. Maybe he had sat at it before, he thought, long ago, a card game with his brother on some rainy summer Sunday.

He came out of the daydream and reached for another cigarette. When he saw there were only three left, he got anxious. He always feared running out. Nevertheless, he had to go into the village to mail some letters and buy dog food. Living out here, with the bad roads and unpredictable weather, he learned it was wise to do all your errands at once.

James continued to type, not sure how long he had even stopped. The truth was, each time he sat down to work, he fell into a mild trance, the content of the letters lulling him into an emotional stupor. He would lose track of time, judging the passing minutes and hours by the cups of coffee, the number of butts in the ashtray.

He stopped, took another drag, and noticed his hand was shaking. He had removed what was obstructing the chimney so he could no longer blame it on the chill. Maybe he was getting sick, he thought, or was deficient in some vitamin or mineral; since arriving in Ireland, his eating had been sporadic. But he was only looking for excuses because the tremor had been with him since he returned from Vietnam a decade before, showing up at different times and in varying degrees. His ex-wife said it was the aftereffects of combat and suggested he seek help or treatment. But James was stubborn, something his mother always reminded him of, and he believed that some wounds just couldn't be healed.

Suddenly, barking.

He got up carefully from the rickety chair—everything in the cottage seemed to be fragile—and went over and opened the door.

"Sonofabitch."

Out in the yard were four cows, standing in a row and eating the neatly stacked piles of weeds like it was a country buffet. All the while Rod circled them, barking fiercely and trying to scare them away. But a small mutt was no match for eight hundred-pound dairy cows, and they ignored him, if they even noticed him at all.

James whistled and Rod ran over, looking up like he didn't know what to do.

"It's okay, boy," he said, reaching down for a dead branch.

As a city boy, James didn't know much about farm animals. The only other time he had been around cows was in the war, the malnourished and flea-ridden breed that roamed the rice paddies, their eyes sunken and ribs protruding. These were completely different, barrel-chested and hearty, and the closer he got, the more astonished he was by their size.

"Scat!" he said.

The first one raised its head, looking back with a dumb curiosity, and the others did the same. If James could tell anything by their expressions, it was that they were annoyed and not intimidated. Rod came over and started to growl until James put out his hand and he stopped. Realizing it would require more prodding, James came up to the first one and whacked it on the rear with the branch.

"C'mon!" he said, waving his arms.

He hit the second, then the third and, to his surprise, the herd slowly began to move. With Rod blocking from one side, James ushered them towards the hedgerows where, one by one, they stepped over the low stone wall and back into the fields. He watched as they went, their powerful hind legs shaking the soft ground, their movements clumsy and yet somehow graceful.

James looked down at the piles of dead vegetation, now scattered and half-eaten.

"I think it's time we get rid of this stuff," he said, and Rod agreed with a yelp.

He went inside for the matches and the fire-starters he bought in the village, small bricks soaked in kerosene that would light under any condition. When he came back out, Rod was waiting eagerly by the refuse like he knew what they were about to do.

"Stand back, boy."

He stuck a few fire starters at the base of each pile and struck a match. Reaching down, he lit them one by one, until the stacks were all burning like funeral pyres. The fire was contained, but the smoke was thick, and James pulled his t-shirt up over his mouth to avoid breathing it in. Rod joined him, and they both stood watching, entranced by the flames and the crackle of the branches. It was over in ten minutes, the dry brush vanishing into circles of black ash, smoldering in places but mostly out.

James flicked his cigarette and looked over to the closest mountain, a treeless mound of scrub grass and rocky ledge, maybe a hundred feet high and a half-mile away by his estimation.

"Whaddya say we go get some fresh air?"

Rod pointed his nose up and barked.

"I'll take that as a yes."

They went out of the yard and up road, and as they passed Tara's house, James noticed her car out front. The place should have made him sentimental, but it bore no resemblance to where his cousins once lived, and he couldn't tell if it had been modernized or simply demolished and rebuilt. Either way, it was much nicer than his shabby cottage, with winter flowers in the window boxes, white lace curtains, and a wreath on the front door.

They came to the end, crossed over the main road, and continued down a small lane barely wide enough for an automobile. They walked through a pasture and started to ascend the hill, following a path that was visible but overgrown. As James examined its course, it didn't seem like the most optimal way up, but he didn't know the terrain and wasn't about to question the wisdom of the shepherds who first made it.

As it started to steepen, his heart pounded and his breathing grew heavy. His knees could handle the incline, but his back was starting to hurt so he leaned forward to relieve some pressure. All the while, Rod scurried around him, and James was impressed by his agility, how he hopped over clumps of grass, scaled rocky outcroppings. James always assumed he was older than him in equivalent years, but the dog had much more energy, and when they were halfway up, he had to stop to rest.

For the first time, James turned around and he was, at once, amazed. The coastline seemed to go on for a hundred miles in either direction, the ocean an infinite stretch of deep blue. All around him were mountains, bare and barren, which descended into valleys of fields and stone walls. The silence was near total, the only sound the soft breeze and that faint but persistent ringing he had had since the war, damage from artillery blasts. James had been walking for just twenty minutes, and yet he felt like he had reached the clouds.

He found a rock that was dry and sat down. His boots were muddy and he was sweating all over, but the air was crisp. As he stared out in a daze, his senses were alive and his mind clear for the first time in weeks. He had come up here with his uncles and cousins, or was he mistaking the mountain for the small hill across the road from the house? He really wasn't sure, and his memories from that time were a mix of what they were and what he wanted them to be. If some of it was fantasy, he didn't care because he cherished those days, and it was a rare thing for the past to be compensation for the present.

James heard rustling and looked over to see Rod with his nose in a gully, digging at the sod with both paws. When he whistled, the dog lifted his head and ran over.

"Whatcha got?"

He grabbed Rod's snout and saw a small metal object between his teeth, about the size of a pebble and heavily corroded. He pulled it out, wiped off some rust flakes, and it was a bullet slug. Rod suddenly began to howl, so loud that James flinched and, for a moment, was even nervous. The dog then rubbed against his leg, whimpering and licking his scarred hand, and James got an eerie feeling. When he spoke, it was almost like he was talking in a dream.

"This the one that killed you?"

Rod stopped and they locked eyes. With a single yelp, he backed away and then ran off to play in the heath. James rubbed his face, swallowing with emotion, his hands trembling, as fragile as he had ever been.

As Tara came over the hill, she heard barking in the distance. She walked along the ridge, sheep scurrying around her, and looked over to see a man sitting down, a dog meandering nearby. She would have avoided him—she only ever came up here to be alone—but she couldn't because he was in the middle of the path. So she continued to walk, stepping carefully over the rutted ground, and as she got closer, she realized it was James. She pushed her hair back and puckered her lips, the feminine ritual she had learned as a girl, so ingrained it was almost a reflex.

She approached slowly, not wanting to startle him, but it didn't help because once the dog noticed her, it began to bark.

"Hello," she said preemptively.

James got up and turned around.

"Fancy seeing you here," he said.

It was his friendliest greeting to date, and she couldn't help but smile.

"What better place on a Tuesday afternoon?"

She walked up and they faced each other in a short but self-conscious silence. She knew James didn't like to talk, or that it was hard for him, and each time she came by the cottage, she felt like she was intruding upon his solitude. But up here, alone among the glens, she didn't need to justify her presence and, for once, she put the burden of conversation on him.

Tara stood quiet and waited until, finally, he spoke.

"Do people hunt up here?"

"Hunt?" she said.

"Hunt...like with rifles."

Tara looked around, glancing up at the sheep on the high ground, surprised the dog wasn't already chasing them.

"There's not much to hunt around here," she said. "Why do you ask?"

"Strange," was all he said, and it wasn't really an answer.

"How are you finding life in Connemara?"

"I'd take less rain."

"Are you bored to tears yet?"

She watched as he smiled, a tight and clumsy smile, like it was difficult to make or he wasn't used to doing it.

"There's enough surprises—"

Just as he said it, Tara noticed a plume of smoke coming from somewhere near the shore. She scanned the coast to get her bearings, and when she did, she was horrified to realize that it was close to their houses.

"Smoke," she gasped, and James looked behind.

"Dammit!"

Without another word, he took off down the hill, and Rod shot after him. Tara followed as best she could, but her legs were shorter, her feet smaller. As a girl, she had broken her ankle diving into a lake, and she didn't want it to happen again. It only took five minutes to reach the base, however, and once she was on level ground, she was able to catch up.

They went by a few scattered homes, came out to the main road, and crossed over, continuing down towards the water. When they passed her house, Tara was relieved to see that it was safe, but smoke was rising over the hedgerows, and she feared for the cottage.

Finally, they both turned into the property and came to a sudden stop.

"Afternoon."

Standing there was a middle-aged man with a gray beard, dressed in a flat cap, knitted wool sweater, and work bib. Across the yard, Tara saw someone raking over the smoldering grass, and when they glanced back, it was one of the boys James had hired to help clear the brush. Rod ran over and stood next to him, barking at the embers, intrigued by the smoking ground.

"I thought it was out," James said.

"Likely was," the man responded, his accent so thick it sounded like he was slurring. "But that gorse there'll burn like a featherbed. Don't take much more than a spark."

"Thank you," James said, hands on his hips, shaking his head.

"Not at all. Lucky me nephew seen it."

When the man looked over towards the water, Tara saw a small fishing boat floating in the shallows, its anchor line running up to the beach.

James reached in his pocket and took out his wallet, and Tara was privately appalled. She had met enough Americans to know they could never accept any assistance or goodwill without payment, as if money was the only form of exchange.

"Now, now," the man said, shooing him away. "None of that. T'was our duty, else you'd have burned the whole headland and us along with it."

James put back the wallet, trying to smile, clearly shaken. Tara didn't know if it was embarrassment or worry, but it was the most emotion she had ever seen from him.

Moments later, the boy walked over dragging the rake, the dog scurrying behind.

"It's out," he said.

The crisis was over, but Rod was still worked up, and he only relaxed after James reached down and patted him. They all stood quietly in the aftermath of the fire, the air filled with the sweet smell of burnt gorse, heath, and scurvygrass. It was hardly a blaze, more like a creeping glow that slowly consumed all the low-lying vegetation and threatened to make its way across the coastal plain. Half of the yard was blackened, some of the perimeter shrubs singed, but overall the damage was minimal, and the property still looked better than before James had started cleaning it up.

"So, you're from Boston?"

James turned to the man.

"What makes you say that?"

"I can hear it in ye accent."

After a short pause, James simply said, "I am."

"I lived there over twenty years meself," the man went on. "Was a pipefitter in Dorchester." He stared intensely, rubbing his chin. "Have we met?"

As he leaned in closer, James seemed to pull back, and it was the first time Tara ever saw him balk.

"I...don't believe so."

"You look mighty familiar," he said, squinting in the harsh afternoon light.

"Boston's a big place."

"Not so big—"

"Uncle," the boy called out, and everyone looked over. "Tide's moving fast."

The winds had started to shift, whitecaps forming out in the bay, and closer to shore the waterline was receding.

"G'day," the man said, tipping his hat.

He beckoned to the boy, and they started to walk, across the grass and towards the bluff.

"Thanks again," James said, almost as an afterthought. "I don't know what would've happened—"

The man raised his arm but didn't look back.

"Nothing burns forever," he said.

Ten

≪⊃

JAMES SQUATTED BY THE CORNER IN A T-SHIRT, HIS PANTS rolled up and boots untied. Every few seconds, he dipped the brush into the paint can and ran it along the wall in long, steady strokes. The cottage had no baseboards like in America so each time he reached the bottom, he had to be careful not to touch the floor. He always thought the parlor had wallpaper but realized he was probably confusing it with his cousins' house—he and his brother spent so much time at both places that the memories blended together. Now he was certain the room was always white, although years of turf smoke and dampness had transformed it into a faint, sickly beige. Except for some cracks and the gouge made from when he threw the typewriter, the old walls were remarkably intact, and he was impressed by the work of the original builders.

James thought back to when his father used to take him and his brother to work on weekends or during school break. Although they were only boys, he taught them everything from demolition to carpentry to plastering. In those days, tradesmen were versatile, and when their father couldn't find an electrician, he would run the wiring himself—if a plumber wasn't available, he would thread and solder the pipes. Everything was so specialized now, James thought, and with an inspection required for every minor home improvement, he was glad to be out of the business altogether.

He stood up and wiped his forehead. His back was sore, and his legs were numb from crouching. As he twisted to stretch, he saw Rod across the room, his eyes peering over his folded legs as he lay curled up beside the fireplace. From the moment the dog smelled paint, he had wanted to help, and he only stayed put after James gave him some food.

James went over and got his coffee, black and cold from sitting. On the table were the two letters he had finished that morning, neatly stacked and with the airmail stamps he bought at the airport the day he arrived. When he couldn't figure out how to align the envelopes in the typewriter, he wrote out the addresses, and it took almost as long as the missives themselves because his injured hand was stiff and unwieldy. Nevertheless, they were done—one to his landlord and one to his accountant—and with each letter he sent, he felt one step closer to being freed from the burdens of his past.

He lit a cigarette and walked over to the window, which he had opened to ventilate the room. Outside, the sky was overcast, a sheet of bluish-gray which hinted that the sun might come out. But James knew enough about the weather out here not to be fooled, and his only hope was that the rain would hold off a few more hours because the humidity would keep the paint from drying.

He felt something against his leg and looked down to see Rod.

"Mind that wall."

The dog peered up, pressing his eyes together like he understood, and James responded with a tender smile. Rod had only been around a couple of weeks, but already James couldn't imagine his days without him, something he at first resisted because he didn't come to Ireland for companionship. But he would never turn him away now, and what he felt for the animal was more than just sympathy—it was comradery. Each time he saw that mutilated ear and scarred nose, he was reminded of his own wounds, and maybe, he thought, that was why he always saw Joel Rodriguez staring back.

Suddenly, Rod barked, and James was startled enough that he almost spilled his coffee.

"Settle down, boy," he said.

He took another puff and was just ready to get back to work when he noticed a car coming down the road. He watched as it approached, slithering behind the shrubs, and moments later Tara's Opel Kadett pulled into the yard.

"Now, what's she want?" he mumbled.

Putting the coffee on the table, he walked over to the door and Rod followed. He opened it as Tara was getting out, and she looked different. Her hair was primped—or had it been cut? She had on makeup, red lipstick, and eyeliner, or maybe he was just noticing it for the first time. James wasn't concerned enough with women anymore to be attuned to the fine details, but standing in her white coat and stylish boots, she looked as pretty as a postcard, and all his indifference went away.

"Hello."

"Howdy," he said.

"Have you fever?"

James winced, gave her a sideways glance.

"How do you mean?"

"You have on a t-shirt," she said and then nodded. "And the window is open."

Before he could reply, Rod squeezed by and ran out to greet her, and James didn't try to call him back.

"I was just touching up some paint," he said.

"What you've done is lovely, really," she said, reaching down to pat the dog. "Not many people would invest their own time to fix up a rental."

He paused for a moment then said, "Well, I've got time."

Tara stood back up, and Rod scurried off to play in the yard. She took a few steps towards him, her boots crunching on the gravel, and James thought he could smell a faint perfume. His heart rate increased as she approached, and he got the strange urge to retreat into the doorway, something he told himself wasn't apprehension.

"Does the cottage have warm memories?" she asked, her head tilted, a sympathetic smile.

The question was simple, the words harmless, but he felt somehow threatened, and he looked across with a cold glare.

"Can I help you with something?" he asked.

Her cheery face melted, and the space around them got suddenly tense.

"I...I was just heading into the village," she said, almost apologetically, "and...wanted to see if you needed anything."

"Well, I don't."

Their eyes locked and she nodded slowly, her expression a mix of confusion and affront. James got a twinge of regret—he never liked to be unkind—but he wanted to be left alone. He was surprised when Tara raised her head, took another step forward, and asked, "You don't need anything? Or you don't need anything *from me*?"

He stood silent, refusing to answer because he didn't feel that he had to explain himself. He thought he had been firm enough, but she was more determined than he realized.

"Mr. Dunford," she said, and it reminded him of how his mother would always say "James" instead of "Jimmy" when she was angry. "May I ask why you've come out here?"

He gazed off into the distance, teeth clenched and struggling to hold back a wave of unexpected emotion. He hated how women could make him feel, how they could elicit those deep, unnerving sentiments which he always took as signs of some hidden weakness. His ex-wife was the only person on earth who could make him cry, something that, strangely, he both loved and resented her for.

James whistled to Rod, who looked up from the bushes and came over, tail wagging and oblivious to it all. Finally, he turned to Tara, and when he spoke, he found it hard to look her in the eye.

"That's my business."

Tara drove along the coast, the windshield speckled with salt spray and gusts whipping across the road, rattling the small car. Conditions outside mirrored her own internal tumult, her mind racing and emotions high after her conversation with James. She couldn't tell whether she was more mad or more upset, but when she came over the hill and pulled into the village, she glanced in the rearview and saw that her mascara was smudged, that she had been crying.

She parked across from Joyce's and sat for a moment, wondering if she had pressed James too hard. Everyone was entitled to privacy, and considering her own situation, she had no right to pry into the lives of others. Still, she would have appreciated more tact, a polite rebuttal or even a clever evasion. On the outside, James could be so harsh, and yet she was sure there was something gentler within. She saw how he had tidied up the cottage, clearing away the overgrowth and painting the window trim. He had taken in a stray dog, feeding it and letting it stay with him. These were not the actions of a heartless crank.

To Tara, what people did meant more than what they said. Maybe she was projecting her own hopes on him—her sister always said she was a bad judge of men. But she wasn't looking for love or romance, and either way, he didn't seem the pairing type. She only sought a human connection, a casual friend, someone to talk with and let her know that, on that windswept stretch of rocky seclusion, she was not entirely alone.

It began to rain. Tiny droplets sheeted across the windshield, obscuring the outside world in a haze of gray blur. Looking in the mirror, Tara wiped her eyes and fixed her mascara. In some ways, she felt silly, dressed for a night in London only to visit a shop in some rural backwater. She wasn't trying to impress anyone, and she only did it for herself. Since coming to live out here, she had forced herself to get dressed up at least once a week, styling her hair and doing her makeup, putting on some of the nicer clothes she otherwise never had occasion to wear. To get through the cold and dreary monotony of her days, it was the one way she could keep her dignity and nurture those last filaments of her ever-fading youth and sensuality. It was all a charade, and she knew as much. But Tara always had a mischievous side, and she couldn't deny that she got some small thrill from the one or two looks she might get from a fisherman or farmhand.

When she stepped into the shop, there was a small crowd over at the bar, men sitting and standing around with pints, smoking hand-rolled cigarettes. They all looked the same in their knit sweaters and wool pants, gray and brown like the landscape around them. Younger people dressed in fashion, of course, Sassoon jeans and Members Only jackets. But with the economy in shambles, most of them had left for big cities

—Dublin or London, Boston or Melbourne—and those who remained were generally older people and families with kids.

The television was on, although no one was watching it, and Tara saw newsflashes about events in the North. Even from two hundred miles away, the images made her feel strangely vulnerable, and she worried for her father and sister. Things had been relatively calm back home, nothing like the chaos of the early '70s, but the British Army still patrolled the streets of Belfast and Derry, and the IRA and Protestant paramilitaries were engaged in tit-for-tat assassinations and sporadic bombings. People went about their daily lives, but everyone knew the country was only one incident away from an all-out civil war.

"What can I get for ye?"

Tara looked up, realizing she had zoned out, and Jerry was at the counter.

"Afternoon, Jerry," she said, regaining her composure and quickly walking over. "Just a quart of milk, half pound of ham, a box of fire starters."

"You know where the fire starters are," he said, nodding towards the shelves. "I'll go out back and see what we have for meat."

"Oh, do you have any soft cheese? Maybe brie?"

"Brie?" someone at the bar snickered.

"Must be a duchess," another remarked.

Tara glanced over with a sour smile, trying to hide her annoyance.

"Pay them no mind," Jerry said under his breath. "I can check."

He walked out back to the refrigerator, leaving her awkwardly alone, hands around her pocketbook. In an area that relied mostly on farming and agriculture, rain could bring the entire workday to a halt, and she knew the men had probably been drinking since noon. She quietly browsed the shelves, her head down and trying to escape their attention. But as the only other person in the shop—and a woman—she knew it wouldn't last.

"On holidays, Miss?"

She looked across to the bar and wasn't sure who asked because they were all staring back.

"Um, no. I live up the road."

"From the North, are ye?" a burly man said.

"Donegal, originally."

It was an answer she had given so many times out here that she almost believed it. Saying she was from a county in the north that was technically not part of Northern Ireland was a convenient way of explaining her accent while avoiding the politics.

Another man looked over, a pint in hand and leaning against the counter.

"Really?" he said. "My granny was from Donegal. Which part?"

She was stumped by the question, which she never would have expected because people around here didn't travel much. Tara could always manage one lie, but a lie to support another lie was too complicated, and she was relieved when Jerry finally came back out.

"A small village, you probably wouldn't know it," she said quickly, then turned to Jerry.

"Now," he said, putting down the milk and showing her a round foil package.

"Lymeswold."

"That'll do, thanks."

"British cheese," someone at the bar said.

Jerry frowned but didn't look over.

"You would know, Sean," he said. "After living in Manchester for thirty years."

When his friends all jeered, she laughed and finally felt more at ease. She didn't mean to be so paranoid, so evasive, and she knew their remarks were just friendly barroom banter.

"Off to somewhere special?" Jerry said, ringing in the items.

"Pardon?"

"You look ready for the Galway Races."

"Just felt like dressing up," she replied.

"We should all do that every now and again."

His voice was gentle and fatherly, and she couldn't help but smile. When the register opened, he looked up and said, "One pound twenty, please."

Tara paid and reached for the bag, glancing over to the men as she turned to go. None of them looked back, however, because they were all gazing at the television. On it, she saw the young face of Bobby Sands, his long auburn hair pouring over his shoulders, his eyes darkened from stress but confident, nonetheless. Imprisoned for his role in an IRA bombing, he was preparing for a hunger strike, and the country was waiting to see how the British would react. As she watched, her body got tense, her breathing grew shallow. Feeling like she was on the verge of panic, she tore her eyes from the screen, grabbed her things, and left.

Outside it was now pouring. Water dripped from the gutters of the small shops, and in the distance, the clouds hung low over the mountains. Tara pulled her hood over her head and ran across the street where, for a moment, she fumbled with her car keys until she realized it was open. Forgetting that she never locked her doors out here was a temporary lapse, brought upon by distrust and the lingering habits from living in places that were not so safe.

She put the bag down on the seat, started the engine, and made a wide U-turn. She sped out of town, veering left at the fork, the wipers creaking. She gripped the wheel and stared ahead, the hedgerows whipping past like the frames of a film reel and lulling her into a dreamy reflection. She thought back to her childhood, recalling a similar dreary day twenty-five years earlier.

Tara saw herself and her sister playing in front of their new house, dressed in the matching raincoats their uncle had brought back from London. It wasn't raining but a constant mist hung over the city, carrying with it the industrial stench of the nearby shipyards. After a year on the waiting list, her family had just moved into a large council estate on the northside of the city. It was an endless network of identical homes, modern and roomy, and far nicer than the two-story brick flat they had lived in since she was born. There were two bathrooms—a luxury by the standards of the time—and Tara and Alice finally each had their own bedroom.

Leaving the warm familiarity of their old neighborhood was scary but also exciting, and the leafy complex was worlds away from the gritty, narrow streets of East Belfast. But they didn't know anyone, and as Alice did cartwheels across the small strip of grass outside their house, Tara noticed two girls and a boy across the street. Her sister stopped and looked too, and for the next few minutes, the two groups eyed each other with that mix of curiosity and suspicion all kids have.

Finally, Alice, who had always been more brash, waved and they walked over, stopping at the curb.

"We just moved here," she said.

"From where?" the older girl asked.

"Belfast."

"This is Belfast," the boy said.

Alice looked up to Tara—the others were similarly confused.

"Another part, then," she said.

For any child, a city was too vast to grasp the differences between districts and divisions, and all the girls knew was that they were a train ride away from where they used to live.

Although the conversation was stilted, it was moving in the right direction, and Tara was hoping for some new friends. But even at age eleven, she could sense an underlying tension, some vague mistrust that she couldn't explain.

"Me mum says you're Prods," the youngest said with a lisp.

The word had the sting of profanity, the force of an accusation. Tara and her sister had heard it a lot before, but they really didn't understand what it meant, and their parents did everything they could to shield them from the ugly bigotry that ran deep in the North.

"What's a Prod?" Alice asked.

Just as she said it, their mother came rushing out of the house with her hair in curlers. She gave the other children a stern look and then told Tara and Alice to get inside. It was the last time they ever talked, watching each other grow up from opposite sides of the street. They went to different schools, attended different churches, played in different sports leagues. The parents were cordial, sometimes even friendly, but like all the families on their cul-de-sac, they wouldn't socialize, and it wasn't long before Tara realized that they had moved into a predominantly Catholic housing estate.

She shivered at the memory of that day and put it quickly out of her mind. As her thoughts drifted back to the present, she looked up. Suddenly—a herd of sheep ahead. She hit the brakes and cut the wheel, careening into a gully and missing a stonewall by just inches. The car finally came to a stop, and she sat still, her heart pounding and shaking all over.

Tara put it in reverse and tried to back out, but the tires spun in the muddy grass.

"For Chrissakes!"

She got out and climbed the embankment, slipping on the rocks, the wind in her face. When she reached the top, she walked out and stood in the middle of the road. She looked around at the barren landscape, the rocky crags and windswept drumlins, and had never felt more alone in her life. Looking down, she saw that her Burberry coat was stained with mud, one of her boot heels broken. She began to cry.

Moments later, she heard something, a steady hum in the distance. She turned around and noticed, through the haze of the rain, a vehicle coming towards her. She waved her arms, and an old Dodge pickup slowed down and stopped.

"Afternoon, Miss."

Tara sighed in relief when she saw the fisherman who had put out the brush fire at the cottage.

"I've gone off the road," she said, shouting over the wind.

He got out and came around the front of the truck, holding his hat so it wouldn't blow off. He looked down at the stranded car and said, "Have ye tried to back it out?"

"The tires just keep spinning."

He turned to her with a reassuring smile, his face tan from days at sea, deep crevices on his cheeks.

"Let's get you home for now. We'll find someone to haul it out later."

"Thank you," she said. "If I could just get my things."

She stepped carefully down into the ravine and got her pocketbook and groceries from the front seat. As she came back up, the man reached over and took her arm so she wouldn't lose her balance. He held open the passenger door, and she got into the small pickup, the fabric seat torn and filthy. It was a workingman's truck, littered with everything from boxes of lures to empty bags of Tayto's.

The man ran around to the driver's side, squinting in the heavy wind, and got in.

"Are ye okay?" he asked.

"I think so."

As they pulled away, Tara looked over at her car and remembered that she left the keys in the ignition, the doors unlocked. She felt a momentary panic until she realized that no one out here would ever steal it anyway.

"Paddy Coyne," he said, introducing himself.

"Tara."

"You're from up north?"

"Um, no. Well, I mean, Donegal formerly," she said, stumbling through the lie that she had now told twice. "But I lived in London for many years."

"What brings ye to Connemara?"

Leaning against the window, she paused and looked out at the gray landscape.

"The weather."

He laughed out loud and then reached for a pipe on the console.

"Don't worry," he said, glancing over. "I just chew on it."

"I see."

"I only light up on weekends. Me wife says it's healthier."

She smiled to herself. In some ways, he reminded her of her father, although they looked nothing alike. Maybe it was his voice, she thought, and she had always been comforted by the gentle baritone of older men.

They came over a shallow hill where in the distance Tara could see her house at the end of the peninsula, a small white fleck amid a thousand shades of green. The cottage was there too, although hidden behind the brush, so close to the shoreline that she sometimes worried a big storm could wash it out to sea. But everything out here was hearty, whether it was the vegetation, the wildlife, or manmade structures, and the land so ancient that anything not equipped to endure would have long since perished. In moments like this, when she was the most exasperated, she found solace in the timelessness of her surroundings, knowing that her own troubles were trivial and temporary.

"I've been thinkin' about your boyfriend."

Startled from her daydream, Tara turned to Paddy.

"Boyfriend?" she said. "You mean James? He's not my boyfriend."

"You seem pretty sure about that."

Their eyes locked, and she detected a hint of sarcasm in his expression. She didn't like being teased about such things, but she conceded with a smile because she realized how defensive she sounded.

"He's just a tenant," she said, lowering her voice. "My auntie owns the property."

"I know I've seen him somewhere before."

"Is that right?"

"In America," he said.

"Maybe you met him in a bar?"

"Doubt it. That I wouldn't forget."

Tara sank into her seat and stared back out the window, water streaming down in chalky streaks, the slurry of windblown sand and soil. Maybe Paddy was mistaken about James, she thought, or maybe it was an intentional fabrication—she learned quickly that people out here liked to tell stories. They were never outright lies but rather the gossip and hearsay of a culture that relied on embellishment to keep life interesting.

Paddy slowed down and turned after the bridge, the truck bouncing over the uneven ground, things creaking in the back. As they approached her house, Tara saw smoke rising from the chimney of the cottage and knew that James was home. He almost never left, spending his days in and around the property, walking over the barren hills and headlands, the dog at his side—always. She was touched by how he treated the animal, caring for it like it was his own, and she only wished he would show her some small fraction of the same courtesy. They didn't have to be friends, and she respected that James wanted to be alone. But the way he spoke to her earlier was almost hostile, and they lived too close to each other to be enemies.

Paddy pulled into the yard and stopped. The rain had lessened to a light sprinkle, a lull in the storm that Tara knew wouldn't last for long. She quickly put on her hood and reached for the door handle.

"Thanks a million," she said as she stepped out.

Paddy raised his unlit pipe like he was toasting a glass.

"Have you a telephone?"

"I don't," she said.

"Then shall I call for a tow truck in the morning?"

"Don't bother, I'll take care of it."

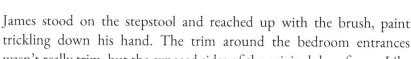

James stood on the stepstool and reached up with the brush, paint trickling down his hand. The trim around the bedroom entrances wasn't really trim, but the exposed sides of the original door frame. Like everything in the cottage, it was dry and cracked, covered by tiny holes that were the handiwork of termites and beetles. Every couple of minutes, he would step down and dip the brush in the can, saturating it so he could fill in the crevices. But the old wood seemed to drink it all up, and the more coats he applied, the more obvious the imperfections, and he just couldn't seem to get the surface smooth.

His eyes watered; his nose hairs tickled. With the constant rain, the parlor still hadn't dried, and the fumes were so strong he had slept the previous night with all the windows open. Nevertheless, it felt good to be painting, something which many people scorned but couldn't do. As a boy, James and his brother did all the hard work for their father, from lugging shingles up ladders to digging holes for cement footings. He learned how to use a hammer before he could use a pencil, and the taste of sawdust was no less familiar to him than oatmeal or cornflakes. Considering all the possible grueling jobs in construction, painting was almost a respite, the meditative back and forth, the solemn sway of the brush.

As he worked, his mind drifted back to those days working for his father, and he smiled in recalling an incident he had forgotten about. They were restoring a three-family house that was gutted by fire, and with the plaster on the new walls barely set, their father left him and his brother alone to do the painting. With the mischievous bent of any teenager, James suggested they write things which they could later cover up, and his brother agreed. They fell into a wild fit of graffiti, some hilarious and some poignant, profanity-laced screeds about teachers they hated, lewd insinuations about girls they liked. It was a blazing hot day, the middle of July, and by the time they were done, the plaster had dried in a way that, even when painted over, showed the words beneath. They were as panicked as they were horrified until his brother pointed out that it was only visible in direct sunlight. When their father finally returned to get them, they were lucky that it was too dark out to see, and for a long time after they laughed about how shocked some future tenant would be on that first bright day.

James heard a noise and startled, almost losing his balance. When he glanced over his shoulder, Rod was looking up, his tongue out and eager for attention. And there beside him, the gallon of trim paint he had knocked over, a lava flow of thick white creeping across the floor.

James jumped down off the stool.

"Outta here! Now!"

Confined by the narrow hallway, Rod scurried backward, his paws slipping on the hardwood, splashing in the paint. James swiped his leg, not intending to hurt him but only to scare him away. Finally turning around, the dog ran through the parlor and out the open front door. James stopped at the threshold, squinting in the gray light of the over-cast afternoon. He watched as Rod scurried off, out of the yard and into the fields, his yellow coat blending into the straw-colored heath until, finally, he was gone.

James tried to call after him but realized it was useless because the dog was frightened, probably confused, and even animals had their pride. He lumbered back inside, his hands sticky and his back sore, and shook his head at the mess, the spilled paint and the frantic swirls of Rod's pawprints. He was more frustrated with himself than the dog, but that regret was quickly replaced by anger. Without thinking, he swung his foot and sent the can flying down the hallway, where it bounced off the wall and rolled into the back bedroom. He stood pant-ing, arms out like he had just knocked down a contender and was waiting for more. James always expected to feel satisfied after an outburst but never was, and his temper was like sex without climaxing.

He got some rags and sopped up the spill, rinsing them in the faucet, the paint congealing in the cold water. He realized he would need another gallon, as well as some turpentine, which was the only thing that would remove the splotches on the floor. So he washed up in the bathroom, grabbed his coat and keys, and headed out to the village.

He cruised easily down the coast, a cigarette in hand and Van Morrison playing softly on the radio. The road ahead and behind was empty for as far as he could see, making him wonder if it was Sunday. At some point, he had lost track of time, the days blending into one another in a seamless and steady procession towards eternity. He no longer saw a need for the distinction, however, and he imagined he was living like the first settlers of this land, rising with the sun and sleeping once it got dark. After living so much of his life bound to the constraints of schedules and routines, he enjoyed the freedom of finally having neither.

Down at the shore, the waves crashed against the rocks, sending up heaps of white spray. The endless cows stood chomping in the fields, their bodies still and tails swaying, fixtures of the landscape. James looked over as he drove, hoping to spot Rod somewhere among them. He wouldn't go after him—the dog would have to come back on his own terms—but he was ashamed of how he had treated the animal and longed to know he was safe.

It had yet to rain, but the mist was heavy, and James turned on the wipers to clear the windshield. As he came over the next hill, he noticed someone walking on the side of the road, and as he got nearer, he was surprised to see Tara. He rolled down the window and pulled alongside.

"Howdy," he said.

She glanced over, but only for a second.

"Hello."

"Everything alright?"

"My car went off the road. I'm going into the village to call for a tow truck."

With her hood on, he couldn't see her face, only wisps of dark hair.

"Can I give you a lift?" he asked.

"No, thank you."

"Where's your car?"

"Just beyond the bend," she said, nodding.

"Let me give you a lift."

"I'll be fine on my own."

Her tone was curt, her attitude cold. He frowned to himself and continued to roll, tapping the throttle a couple of times because it was obvious that she was walking faster. He had frightened Rod and been rude to her, and regardless of his own petty hang-ups, there was no honor in mistreating animals or women.

"I know I was little harsh yesterday," he said.

Tara finally stopped and turned to him.

"A little harsh? You were a right bastard."

James flinched at her words, even felt insulted. But as stubborn as he was, he knew deep down that she was right. And the outburst reminded him that giving scorn was a whole lot easier than receiving it.

"Look," he said. "I was tired."

She shook her head, her face damp, eyelashes wet with mist.

"If this is an apology, Mr. Dunford, it's a damn pathetic one!"

She stormed off and left him idling on the road. He put the car in gear and continued ahead, catching up to her in seconds.

"I'm sorry. Okay?" he said.

Tara veered towards the grass and went down a shallow embankment where, in the distance, James could see her car. He pulled over and got out, looking around and trying to imagine how she went off the road. The back tires were sunk in the muck, but the vehicle was by no means stranded, and he was sure he could get it out.

"I can help," he said.

She ignored him and reached in the car, coming back out and holding up something he couldn't see.

"I needed to get the keys, that's all."

He scurried down the gully, stepping carefully over the wet and rocky turf.

"Just let me try."

"Trust me, it's stuck," she said firmly.

Before she could protest, James began pulling up clumps of grass, weeds, and dead branches. He knelt down and stuffed it all under the tires, pushing it deep into the treads, his hands black with mud. Looking back over his shoulders, he said, "Why don't you go wait in my car?"

She shook her head, her arms crossed and watching with a curious pout. He gathered some more vegetation, and by the time he was done, it looked like she had run over a bale of hay.

"That's some improvising," she said, finally.

James came over to her, out of breath, and wiped his hands on his jeans.

"We used to do this in the war when the jeeps got stuck," he said, then he turned to her. "Keys?"

She handed them to him, and when their hands touched, her skin was cold and clammy. James forced a smile, holding it long enough for her to give in and finally smile back. He didn't know if she forgave him, but her expression softened, and it seemed a step in the right direction.

He walked down to the car, and as he crouched to get in, he was tempted to apologize for the dirt. He started the engine, letting the clutch out slowly so the treads would catch the weeds. And once they did, he hit the gas and the Opel Kadett leapt forward, out of the quagmire and onto more stable ground. He glanced in the rearview, grinning to himself, and he saw a similar excitement on Tara's face. He drove up the embankment, parked on the side of the road, and got out. As he held open the door for her, it began to sprinkle so she hurried over.

"Thank you," she said.

"Drive slow."

She looked up with a faint smile, spoke with a quiet humility.

"I will."

Once she was in, James gently shut the door. She put it in gear, waved through the glass, and sputtered down the long and empty road. The sprinkle turned quickly to rain, but James stood undeterred, thinking about her and watching as the car vanished into the mist. He got a strange and sudden elation like his entire body had been filled with helium, and for the first time in months, maybe years, he experienced what he could only describe as happiness. He didn't know if it was her or that universal satisfaction everyone gets from helping someone in need. Either way, he admired her pluck, walking for miles alone to get her car, and he always liked a woman who was self-sufficient.

Even as it began to pour, James remained in the road, his hair soaked and water seeping into the collar of his coat. It was a cold rain, but he didn't care because inside he was warm, and he didn't want the feeling to go away.

Tara leaned over the sink, her sleeves pulled up as she cleaned the mud off her leather boots. She felt foolish for wearing them, and if the long walk to get her car proved anything it was that they were made for fashion and not durability. The heel on one of the boots was chipped; the toes on both were scuffed. As she wiped them down, she stared at the soft leather, once stiff but now broken in by time and wear. She had owned them for many years, stuffed into the tiny closet of her London apartment along with her suede clogs, Puma tennis shoes, various pumps, and sandals. She once had a pair of Mojari loafers Kevin got for her at a Bangladeshi shop in Notting Hill. Made of gold felt and dotted with fake emeralds, they were too gaudy for her tastes, and the flat soles hurt her feet. Yet Tara wore them for a whole summer because she didn't have the heart to tell him, the same courtesy he showed her when he wore the embroidered Kurtha shirt she bought him at the Stonehenge Free Festival. Their life together was like that, she thought, a host of small tradeoffs and sacrifices, sometimes inconvenient but never not worth it.

Tara came out of a daydream, her elbows on the sink, the water running. She didn't know how long she had drifted, but she was cold and irritable. Beyond that, she was angry with herself, and she had learned early on that the best way to maintain her sanity was to not think about him.

She turned off the tap and set the boots to dry on the counter. By now the sun was down, and just the sight of the dark, barren landscape through the window gave her a chill. She turned on the baseboard heaters, which didn't give off much heat, and the most they would do was keep her from freezing to death. She tried to start a fire but discovered that she had no kindling, and Joyce's was closing soon. So she decided to walk over to the cottage, hoping that if James had been kind enough to help with her car, maybe he would give her a few fire starters to stay warm.

Tara stepped outside and the frigid wind hit her like an electric shock. Nevertheless, she crossed her arms and proceeded into it, down the dark road, the only sound the rush of the waves. She got to the cottage in seconds and was relieved to see James' car, although she would have been surprised if she didn't. As she went through the yard, she was tempted to turn back, and after the way he treated her last time, she didn't want to trouble him.

But Tara refused to be afraid of James so she continued on, stopping within a few feet of the door. Standing there, she recalled that it was the same spot where she first met him, two or three weeks before. Or had it been longer? In the endless tedium of the winter gloom, time was an elusive thing, and the only thing she knew was that her life out here was divided into two very distinct periods, before and after he arrived.

"Try the knocker."

Tara jumped, spun around. It took her eyes a moment to adjust, but when they did, she saw James sitting over by the flower garden, his cigarette glowing.

"Are you trying to scare me to death?" she said.

"The cold will do that quicker."

"I beg your pardon."

"Where's your coat?"

When she suddenly realized she wasn't wearing one, she was as embarrassed as she was concerned. She always seemed to be forgetting things, whether it was a towel when she took a shower or her wallet when she went into the village, and she felt like she was living in a state of constant distraction.

"I knew I'd only be a few minutes," she said, an odd and delayed explanation.

James dropped his cigarette and stamped it on the ground. As he came over, she heard huffing and looked to see the silhouette of Rod in the darkness.

"Hello, love," she said, kneeling to pat him. "So matted."

"He was gone a couple days."

"I wonder where to?"

"Who knows."

"Are you surprised he came back?" she said, standing back up.

"Maybe a little."

Tara looked down at the dog and then to James, who seemed unusu-ally calm, almost reflective, as if she had interrupted him in prayer. She noticed also that she wasn't anxious in his presence, and the gaps in their conversation were now more like valleys than canyons. Maybe their spat on the coast road was a turning point, or maybe the weeks were just wearing down his defiance. All she knew was that no two people could be in the same predicament for too long without feeling a certain solidarity in living.

"Can I help you with something?" he said.

It was the same question as before, only this time it was sincere and not snide, and she was surprised how much of a difference tone and intention could make.

As she looked up to him, his face was obscured by shadows, a fitting metaphor for the mystery that he was. She had only come by for a favor, but in the solemn quiet of the pitch-black night, she got the urge for more.

"I...wanted to know if you'd like to come over for dinner."

"Sure," he said, as quickly as she had asked.

Tara smiled and nodded, pleased that he accepted but in no way prepared.

"Lovely," she said. "Say, half eight?"

"I'll be by at eight-thirty."

"Terrific."

"Look forward to it..."

Their dialogue sputtered out with all the awkwardness of a first date. But it wasn't a date, Tara told herself, just a shared meal with a neighbor, and for her, the prospect of romance seemed as distant and remote as her old life in London. She was open to it, of course, and it was never about staying faithful to Kevin because she knew he would want her to move on. But in the last eighteen months Tara hadn't gone on a single date, and about the closest she had gotten to a man was the time she had a root canal in Galway.

When James called to Rod, she turned to go but not before remembering the reason why she came by.

"Oh, would you happen to have any fire starters? I'm completely out."

James pulled the razor down his cheek, watching in the mirror as the edges of his beard became sharp and clear. He always hated shaving, even as a young man, the numbness of the skin and the occasional nicks.

During the war, he had gone months without it, coming out of the bush looking like a Gray-shanked douc, the men often joking it was part of their camouflage. Nevertheless, his mother had taught him and his brother good manners, and even if he wasn't trying to impress Tara, she deserved the courtesy of a good presentation.

He ran the blade under the cold water, clearing off the stubble, and then wiped his face with a towel. He slapped some cologne on his neck, the bottle of Brut his ex-wife had bought him years before, still full. He put on his white button-down shirt, the closest thing he had to dress clothes, and his cleanest pair of jeans. Finally, he opened his suitcase and reached under all the folded jerseys, underwear, pants, and shirts. He found one of the tins of Café Vienna he had brought from Boston just in case they didn't sell instant coffee in Ireland.

James came out ready, and Rod was cuddled in front of the fire, his food and water bowls beside him.

"C'mon, boy," he said.

He turned the damper on the fireplace, lowering the flame to save fuel and because, after the brush fire, he didn't want to start another one. He put on his coat, grabbed a handful of fire starters, and headed out, Rod following behind. The air was cold but the wind had died down, and he was able to light his cigarette with a single match.

When he turned into Tara's yard, all the lights were on, the curtains open, and it looked as inviting as a Christmas party. Unlike the cottage, the house had been modernized, with a corrugated roof, casement windows, aluminum downspouts, and floodlights. Aside from its general shape and location, it looked nothing like the place where his aunt and uncle used to live. Even so, James began to remember things, like the time his cousin Maggie fell from the pear tree and broke her wrist, or when his brother smashed a bee's nest with a rock and they all ran. Once they found a baby lamb tangled in the barbed wire fencing, its skin sheared to the bone and its mouth bloody. While their cousin Owen ran to get help, James stood captivated, his brother crying uncontrollably at his side. Maybe it was because they were so young, he thought, but that image still haunted him as much as anything he saw in Vietnam.

He walked up to the front door, and just as he went to knock, it opened.

"Hello," Tara said.

She was dressed in a blue blouse, rolled-up jeans, and wool socks without shoes.

"Howdy," he said.

She looked down, and he watched her expression change when she saw Rod.

"You brought...him?"

"Do you mind?"

"Not at all," she said, but something told him she was only being polite. "Please, come in."

James stepped inside the house which, despite all the cheerful light, was bitter cold. Something was cooking, a roast or maybe a stew, its savory aroma reminding him that he hadn't eaten since breakfast. He handed her the fire starters and held out the coffee tin.

"I brought this too."

Tara took it in both hands and looked at it.

"Irish Mocha Mint," she said. "Thank you."

"Ever have it?"

She tilted her head, rolled her eyes.

"Can't say that I have."

She went over to the fireplace, which was against the interior wall like in the cottage. The layout of her house was similar too, James thought, but the rooms were much larger, the ceilings higher. The parlor looked more like an American living room, with a leather couch and walnut coffee table, and the only thing missing was a television. Over by the window was a bookcase, filled from end to end, and beside that a club chair and a floor lamp with an oval shade.

As Tara knelt to light the fire, James quickly said, "Here, let me do that—"

She glanced back with the same sharp look his ex-wife used to give him whenever he tried to help her with something that she was fully capable of doing. His mother had always hated feminism, which was probably why he never considered it, and he expected more modesty from an Irish girl anyway.

"Okay," she said, getting up. "I'll go check on dinner."

James arranged the turf briquettes, stacking them into a pyramid and sticking fire starters in between. Even before it was lit, Rod came over and laid down on roughly the same spot as in the cottage. James reached in his pocket for a match, struck it on the mantle, and tossed it on the pyre. The kindling caught immediately, and the blaze got underway.

He stood up, wiped his hands, and looked over towards the kitchen, where Tara was taking a pan out of the oven. She knelt with the grace of a curtsy, knees together and toes pointed. Her jeans hugged her body, accentuating the shape of her hips and curves of her legs, and he understood why his old-fashioned mother always scorned them on young women.

"I hope you like ham," she said, suddenly turning around. "I didn't even think to ask."

James averted his eyes like he had been caught gawking then walked over to the bookshelf.

"Love it," he said.

He browsed the titles, paperbacks and hardcovers, most of them old, worn, and dusty. There were novels, biographies, recipe books, and even an Irish dictionary, a language that everyone was nostalgic for but no one spoke.

"Have you read any of these?"

"Afraid not," she said as she spooned roasted potatoes into a dish. "Too distracted these days."

"Out here?"

She stopped, looked up, and their eyes met.

"I've just...had...a lot going on," she said with a wistful smile, and James took it to mean more. "Ready to eat?"

He walked over and she motioned for him to sit. The kitchen table was contemporary and well-built, much sturdier than the one in the cottage, and he could rest his arms without worrying about knocking something over. He looked at the sliced ham, roasted carrots and potatoes, cheese and crackers, and realized he hadn't had a solid meal in weeks. Since he arrived, James had been living off scrambled eggs and bacon, toast and potato chips, coffee and Fresca. It was a bachelor's diet that he knew probably would have killed him if it weren't for all the exercise he was getting by fixing up the property and walking several miles each day.

Before she sat, Tara got a bottle of wine off the counter and opened it. She went to pour some in his glass, and he held out his hand.

"None for me, thanks."

"You don't like red?"

"Water is fine," he said nervously.

She pulled the bottle away, filled her glass to the top, and sat down. They passed around the food, and for the first few minutes, they ate in silence, the only sound the crackle of the fire.

"So," she said, finally. "What's life like in Boston?"

"Right now? Cold and snowy. Have you been?"

Tara put her hand over her mouth, swallowed before answering.

"Never to the States. Can you believe it?"

As James reached for some cheese and crackers, he glanced over to see Rod sleeping by the hearth. The fire was burning nicely, and the house was starting to warm up.

"This cheese is delicious," he said.

"Lymeswold. It's British."

"Didn't you live in England?"

"London," she said, nodding. "I was reared in Belfast." She paused and took another sip of wine. "But I don't tell too many people."

He winced, genuinely curious.

"Yeah? Why is that?"

"Well, you know, with all that's going on."

"The IRA prisoners?"

"That, of course—"

"I read there might be a hunger strike."

"It's more than that," she said with a sigh. "This has been going on forever."

James didn't know much about the conflict in Northern Ireland, except that it was always in the local news and always on TV. In the neighborhood he grew up in, everyone was vaguely aware of The Troubles, mainly because most people were first- and second-generation Irish. Still, as an American, it was tough to understand the historic animosity between two groups that seemed so much alike, and he would have been hard struck to explain the difference between a Catholic and a Protestant.

"So," Tara said. "What do you do in Boston?"

"Construction."

"Explains why you like to fix things up."

He gave a slight smirk.

"I like to keep busy, that's all."

She finished her wine and refilled the glass. Her face looked red, but James couldn't tell if it was from her makeup or the alcohol.

"You said your father was a builder. Do you work with him?"

"He died when I was..." He caught himself before he said it—he didn't want to mention the war. "...younger."

"Well, my auntie will be thrilled by all the work you've done."

"It's nothing, really."

"I'll have to tell her."

"Does she live nearby?"

"An elderly care facility up north," Tara said. "That's why I'm here, to keep an eye on things."

"That's good of you."

With her elbows on the table, the glass in one hand, she shifted in the chair like she couldn't get comfortable.

"After my husband passed," she went on. "I needed to get away—"

"How'd he die?"

She looked up, her expression stiff like she didn't expect the question.

"Heart attack."

"I'm sorry."

James meant it sincerely, but he didn't entirely believe her—something in the response sounded flat and rehearsed. He learned young how to detect bullshit, a skill that was further honed while in the military, where honesty and loyalty were two sides of the same ideal. But he didn't question her, or push the subject, knowing that, like most people, her past was probably complicated, and they each had their own reasons for coming out to Connemara.

After they finished eating, Tara got up and started to clear the table.

James tried to help, but she wouldn't let him so he sat and watched as she gathered the plates, dishes, and silverware and put them in the sink. With the wine bottle empty, she got more from the cabinet, another red but with a different label.

"Sure you won't have a glass?" she asked, looking over.

"No, thanks."

"I wish I had some beer," she said as she pulled out the cork. "But I do have whiskey—"

"I'll stick with water."

"Shall we move the party to the sitting room?"

He nodded, and when he got up from the chair, Rod lifted his head and looked over. As they made their way towards the couch, Tara stumbled on the floorboards and giggled. They sat down on the couch, and she got closer than he expected, curling one leg beneath her, running her arm along the cushions. James was never self-conscious around women, but they could make him uneasy, especially when they were drinking. And if he knew anything about alcohol, it was that it could make things go either really good or really bad.

"Beautiful house," he said.

"Much different than you remember it, I'm sure."

"You could say that."

He looked around and saw a picture frame on the side table. In it was a man, woman, and two young girls, all dressed in swimsuits and smiling on a wide beach, the sand white and dotted with umbrellas. Although in color, it had the pasty hues of older photographs, and James guessed that it was from the Fifties.

"Is that your family?"

He felt foolish for asking because it obviously was. But she obliged him, moving even closer and gazing at the picture with a poignant smile.

"My sister Alice," she said. "My mother, my father."

"I never knew Ireland had beaches like that."

"They don't," she said, reaching for her glass and taking a sip before answering. "That was taken in Spain. I was probably ten. My sister, three."

"You were both blonde."

"Alice still is," Tara said, touching her hair, running the strands between her fingers. "Not sure what happened to me."

James grinned and looked again at the picture.

"You don't look much alike."

"We aren't. Alice was still a girl when The Troubles started. I was in my last year of college. I left for London the minute I could. We've spent most of our lives apart. Sometimes I feel awful about it."

"You did what you had to do."

Tara put down the glass, now almost empty, and pulled both legs onto the couch. She faced him from a distance that was growing increasingly narrower, and he liked the smell of her perfume.

"And what of your family?" she said, her voice soft.

"My family? You already know my father is deceased. My mother lives on Cape Cod."

"Any brothers or sisters?"

"Um, just a brother," he said.

"Does he live in Boston too?"

"I think...I don't...we don't talk."

James started to feel warm, his face flushed and back sweaty, and it wasn't entirely from the heat. He hated thinking about his brother, which in the former home of his aunt and uncle was a hard thing to avoid.

"I'm sorry," she said. "Is he your only sibling?..."

He stared across at the fireplace and simply nodded.

"...Why don't you two talk?"

James cringed inside, but she had every right to ask so he cleared his throat and spoke.

"We worked together...for my father. When he died, I was overseas... in Vietnam. My brother ran the business, made himself president." He spoke in short, scattered sentences like he was recalling a past trauma. "When I got back, I wasn't happy about it. The company was supposed to be split between the two of us. He claimed he built it up while I was gone, said I wasn't entitled to an equal share—"

"Was that your father's wish?"

James shook his head.

"He died young, didn't leave a will. I stayed with the company a few years, but when things didn't work out, my brother fired me. There was nothing I could do."

"Nothing?"

"I tried to sue, but it's dragged on for years. I've decided to cancel it. I'm tired of fighting."

As he sat mesmerized by the flames, Tara uttered something he didn't hear, an apology for his misfortunes or an encouraging phrase. He appreciated the support but didn't want her sympathy because he wasn't a victim. Or if he was, he thought, he was a casualty of the world.

"James?"

Hearing her voice, he came out of the daydream. Just as he turned, she crept forward and pressed her lips to his.

"Wait...what?"

He put out his arms, fending her off with a delicate nudge, and Tara backed away and stood up.

"What is wrong with you?" she said.

"What's wrong with me?"

"I invite you over, we have a lovely dinner—"

"And we did."

"Then what's so wrong about...this," she said, looking at the couch like she wasn't quite sure about her intentions.

"I came out here to be alone."

"You *are* alone!" she shouted, and James stood up. "We're both out here *alone*, in this God-forsaken stick of land..."

He could tell she was drunk, but her words were no less heartfelt, and he was conflicted, realizing he had never turned a woman down before.

"...I won't ask any more about your past," she went on, throwing her arms up. "Or why you're here. But for feck's sake, why can't we make the best of it?"

Rod got up and came over, his tail wagging uncontrollably, as anxious as a child who sees his parents fighting. And it was enough to calm Tara down because the moment she saw the dog, she shook her head and sighed.

"This is so damn humiliating."

She picked up the empty wine glass and went over to the kitchen.

"Who's gonna know?" he said.

"I'm gonna know."

James just stood and watched as she turned on the faucet and started to scrub the dishes. He was sorry they argued, but after living for so long in a stupor, it was just nice to finally feel something again.

"Look," he said. "You're beautiful..."

With her back to him, she nodded but didn't reply.

"...but I can't get involved. It ain't fair to you."

She dropped her head, nodded again, and although he couldn't see her face, he was sure she was either crying or trying not to.

"Just go, please," she said.

He waited to see if there was more, and when there wasn't, he called for Rod. He took one last look at Tara, who remained still, unwilling to look back. With her long hair pouring over her shoulders, she was indeed beautiful, and he would never regret saying it. But James also realized that, like him, she was damaged, and he had seen enough heartache to know that two broken people didn't equal a fixed one. He gestured to Rod, and together they walked out into the night.

Eleven

THE SKY WAS OVERCAST AS TARA DROVE ALONG THE N2 towards Galway. To her left, the mountains were gray masses that created the illusion of shadows in the valleys between them. There was no sunlight, however, and she was thankful for it because she had a horrific hangover, the worst in years, so jarring that she wondered if, beyond making her drunk, the wine had also poisoned her.

By the time she got to the city, the three Paracetamols she had taken were beginning to work, and her head no longer throbbed. The streets were busy in the late-morning rush and, for once, she was comforted by all the activity. She was losing her tolerance for rural life, and there were days she felt like she was going crazy from the tedium. And maybe she was, she thought, because she never would have come on to a man who was so resistant to affection, friendship, love.

Tara was embarrassed, and even a little bitter, but she couldn't blame James for the way he reacted the night before. She would have given herself to him entirely and not because she was tipsy. She had finally met someone more disillusioned by life than herself, something that both frightened and fascinated her, and in some ways, her desire to get through to him was a way to better understand herself.

❧

"I'm Doctor McGrath."

When Tara went to stand, the man put out his hand and urged her to stay seated.

"Pleased to meet you," she said.

"Do you go by Gwendolyn or Gwen?"

"Gwen is fine."

The room was small, with bare white walls, two chairs, and an examination bed. It had an antiseptic odor that made Tara nauseous, and the white lights were starting to resurrect her headache. She wasn't used to medical clinics, having never been sick much, but it made her think of the time her parents took her and her sister to get vaccinated during a polio outbreak.

The doctor took the chair beside her, a clipboard and pen in hand, and she tried not to shake as he reviewed the intake form.

"We didn't find your name in the IHC," he said.

"I've not registered yet. I only moved here last summer."

"From up North?"

The fact that the doctor said *up North* and not *Northern Ireland* was some indication of his political views, but she knew that most people in the Republic supported unification anyway.

"Originally,' she said. "I lived in London for years."

He gave a long nod, put the clipboard down, and turned to her.

"Now," he said. "You've been feeling gloomy?"

Tara grinned to herself and probably would have laughed if it wasn't rude. *Feeling gloomy.* The phrase reminded her of how her mother used to speak, the euphemisms of a generation that, with two world wars and a depression, probably suffered more sadness and anxiety than any before or since.

"My nerves have been particularly on edge."

The doctor smiled warmly and looked back at the form. Although a decade older, something about him was reminiscent of James; maybe it was his long sideburns.

"It says here you lost your husband?"

"Yes, eighteen months ago," she said.

"And how'd he pass?"

Tara hesitated, grasping her pocketbook just enough to give her comfort without making it obvious.

"He died in a work accident."

The doctor scribbled something down and moved on.

"Any trouble sleeping?"

"Most nights," she said.

"Have you had any dark thoughts?"

Their eyes locked for a tense moment.

"How do you mean?"

"Thoughts of taking your own life?"

The room seemed to go suddenly silent—Tara could hear her heart beating in her ears. As the doctor sat waiting, it took every last ounce of nervous energy to not tell him the truth.

"Never."

She was relieved when he accepted the answer and turned back to his notes. She had passed the interview, or was it an interrogation? Either way, she felt guilty because she had, in fact, thought about killing herself many times. The urge was strongest in the months following Kevin's death, but during that period she was too frazzled to make an omelet, let alone carry out a successful suicide. What scared her more now were the fragile moments, those stretches of deep and persistent sadness, when she was emotionally fraught and yet still could function. It was then that she felt the most vulnerable because she knew she could actually do it.

"This is for your nerves," the doctor said, reaching in his smock for a notepad. "You're to take it only as necessary." He glimpsed up and gave her a stern look. "Never any more."

"I understand."

"Get this filled at the chemist across the road."

He tore the prescription slip from the pad and stood.

"Feel better, Ms. Evers."

Tara smiled in thanks and he walked out, leaving a void in the room that she could almost see. She hated when people left, even strangers, because it reminded her how small her world was, how tenuous her connections. There was a time when she had more friends than she could count, those hectic days of her twenties when she worked as a manager at a bank in London. It was around that time that she met Kevin, who came in one Friday afternoon with a rowdy group of laborers, all dressed in work clothes and covered in dust. When he didn't have adequate identification, the teller sent him over to talk with her, and immediately they noticed each other's accent, which led to a casual conversation. They were both from Belfast, although opposite sides of the city, and it was always comforting to talk with someone from home.

Tara technically shouldn't have approved the transaction, but she did anyway, and as she handed Kevin back his check, their hands touched, their eyes met. She could tell he wanted to say more, and she hoped he would, but he was hesitant. Then the moment before he turned to go, before he disappeared forever into the anonymity of the city, he stopped and spoke. *I'll be at The Tipperary this evening. Fleet Street. Won't you come by?*

Thinking back now, those next few seconds changed the course of her life. At first, she was reluctant to say yes and not because she wasn't interested. He had a nice smile, a gentle manner, and enough confidence to be charming without seeming cocky. But being from the same war-torn city had its own complications, and she wasn't sure she could take the risk. Tara didn't just leave Belfast so much as escape it, and despite some lingering homesickness, she wanted to put all that behind her.

"Miss?"

When she looked up, a nurse was standing in the doorway.

"So sorry," she said, quickly collecting herself and getting up.

"It's just that we've got patients."

"Of course."

Tara rushed down the hallway and through the front lobby, where mothers with young children were waiting to be seen. It was the height of the flu season, and the entire country seemed to be coughing, sniffling, wheezing, and weary. In some ways, she envied them, knowing that those were the illnesses of social interaction and community. Living on the remote shoreline, safe from all those pathogens, Tara hadn't had a cold all winter.

She walked out front and stopped on the sidewalk. She had lived for months with the quiet shame of her mental state and was relieved to finally tell another person about it. But the doctor wasn't a psychotherapist, and she was far from healed.

Tara looked across the street to the chemist then down at the slip in her hand. Her parents had always scorned medicine for anything other than physical ailments, believing that matters of the mind and emotions were the domain of the church. So she got a chill when she read the small word scribbled in black ink: Valium.

Twelve

As James drove along the coast road, Rod sat nervously beside him, fidgeting on the stiff vinyl seat, and it was obvious he had never been in a car before. But he learned fast, stabilizing his hind legs and leaning to the sway of the long and winding contours. James admired his resilience, knowing that any dog who had survived the wild could adapt to the ways of society. He always respected animals more anyway, and even as a young boy he sensed an honor in nature that was absent from humanity. It was never kind and often brutal, but there was no envy, hatred, revenge.

"Hang on, boy."

They followed a sharp curve up the hill, and James slowed as they entered the village. The narrow two-lane road was busy, a milk truck blocking one side, and it was the closest thing to a traffic jam he had seen in Ireland. Instead of waiting for a spot, he turned into the service station, the only one for miles, and he realized that he hadn't needed gas in weeks. There were two pumps—one for regular and one for diesel—both worn and rusted. An attendant in overalls strolled over, opened the cap, and started to fill it before James could say how much he wanted. Once finished, the man asked if he could pay in dollars because he "liked the look of them American notes," and James obliged him with his last ten.

As he pulled out, a space opened in front of Joyce's and he shot across, sending Rod scrambling to find his footing.

"Wait here," he said, rubbing him under the chin.

When James walked in, everyone at the bar turned, and he felt like a lone gunslinger entering a saloon. But he wasn't a threat, and he wasn't a stranger, and since moving out to the cottage, he had been coming by the shop at least twice a week for groceries and to get his mail. He didn't mind curiosity, but he despised nosiness, and when he found the men looking longer than necessary, he stared back with a cold glare.

They all went back to their pints, grumbling amongst themselves until a news bulletin came on TV and got everyone's attention. It was more about The Troubles, that much James knew, scenes of Catholic protesters marching in the streets, tense discussions between Unionist and Republican politicians, and the IRA bombing of a British coal ship. Before, he might have dismissed the conflict, and compared to what he had seen in the Sixties—Vietnam, race riots, political assassinations, student unrest—it was like a backyard squabble. But knowing that Tara had grown up among all that hostility made him think differently, and he realized that every war had its victims, no matter how large or small.

"Afternoon."

James looked over to see Jerry behind the register.

"I need tap nails?" he said.

"Tap nails? How many?"

"A couple dozen, I'd say."

"Let me check."

Jerry turned around and opened a cabinet filled with hardware—brackets and clamps, screws and hooks, doorknobs and lubricating oil. As he searched, James went over to the shelves and got a loaf of bread, potatoes, some currant jam, and a small bag of dry dog food. He took it all over to the counter, and Jerry held up a box.

"They only come in packs of fifty."

"That's fine," James said.

"Want your mail too?"

When he nodded, Jerry walked over to a cubby with a sign that said *An Post* over it and looked through the slots.

"I've got something for your neighbor too," he said. "She's not been in for a few days. Would you take it?"

James hesitated—it took him a moment to realize he meant Tara.

"Um...sure."

Jerry bagged the items, putting the mail on top, and rang everything in. James paid, and when he walked out, he was surprised to see someone leaning against his car. Noticing the man also had his arm in the window, he flew into a rage and ran over, ready to shove him away or worse.

"Get the hell away from him!"

The man looked up, a pipe hanging from his mouth. James saw it was the fisherman who had put out the fire at the cottage and instantly composed himself.

"Sorry, I didn't realize it was you."

"That's a friendly pup you have there," the man said, oblivious to the outburst.

"I wouldn't say he's *mine*. He showed up at my door."

"Well, I never seen him before you arrived, me nephews neither."

James gazed through the glass at Rod, who sat still on the seat. The dog suddenly looked back, like he knew he was being watched, and James got a chill.

"Is that right?" he said, opening the hatch of the car.

"But I seen you before..."

James put the grocery bag in the back, only half-listening and not interested in small talk.

"...in the Boston newspaper."

He froze. James had come to Ireland for anonymity, and the fact that someone thought they knew something about him made him feel exposed.

"You won that big medal," the man said.

"Medal?"

James slammed the hatch down hard, and the man followed him around to the car door.

"For the war," he went on. "I remember."

As James crouched to get in the small Toyota, he tempered his annoyance with a tight smile. Like any rural place, the village was a hotbed of gossip and rumor, and when he saw two old ladies stop on the sidewalk, he knew the conversation was attracting attention.

James started the car and, the moment before he shut the door, he looked up to the man and spoke with a friendly but firm directness.

"You must have me confused with somebody else."

James turned off the main road, a cigarette between his teeth, and drove carefully so the groceries in the back didn't spill. He hated the tiny cars in Ireland and missed the spaciousness of his '76 Cutlass coupe. On rougher surfaces, the Toyota was like riding a skateboard over a rockpile, and each time he saw a rut, he would slow almost to a halt, cringing as he went over it and waiting for the bottom to scrape. His dread was less about damaging the rental and more about the sound because since the war he had lost all tolerance for grating noises.

He came around the bend and up ahead saw the three boys from the other side of the hill, standing in a circle and examining something on the ground. The only way he knew it was a weekday was because they had on uniforms, and they must have recently got out of school. As he approached, they all turned and moved to the side.

"Howdy," he said, and they all replied, "Hello, sir."

James put his cigarette in the ashtray and leaned out to see the carcass of a small animal in the grass, wet with blood and mangled beyond recognition.

"A hare," one of the boys said before he could ask.

"He get run over?"

"A dog," the oldest boy said. "We think."

James glanced once more at the body, shook his head, and put the car in gear. As he started to roll, he remarked, "Careful or you'll get rabies."

"No rabies in Ireland, sir."

James tapped the brake, looking in the side-view mirror, where the boys stood huddled, arms at their sides. Despite all his knowledge and life experience, they knew more about the habitat than he ever would, and he respected their young wisdom. Growing up in the city, James' childhood was a self-contained world of brick and asphalt, the only vegetation weeds and the worn-out grass of overused parks. Aside from dogs, cats, and squirrels, he hadn't even seen another wild animal until his parents took him and his brother to the zoo when he was twelve.

James waved as he drove away, and the boys all waved back. He drove down the road, around another slight bend, and in the distance, the sea was dark aqua, the islands hovering at the horizon in a dull fog that merged with the low-lying clouds. He turned into Tara's yard reluctantly and pulled behind the Opel Kadett. He grabbed her mail, a single letter whose return label he had, up until then, not noticed:

Alice Evers
   13 Parker Street, Belfast
   United Kingdom

It struck him that the address was England and not Ireland, something he always knew in theory but never thought about, and it seemed strange for two countries to occupy one island. He may not have understood the politics that caused it, but he knew about fear and distrust, and Boston was no less provincial, a patchwork of small fiefdoms separated by race, nationality, and social class. When the first Puerto Rican family moved into his neighborhood, their windows were smashed, their kids harassed at school. The oldest son, Ramon, died in Vietnam the same time James was there, although he didn't find out until he got home.

James walked across the front yard, his boots crunching on the gravel, and stopped at the door. After what had happened between Tara and him, he should have been flattered, but instead, he felt remorse. Maybe he should have obliged her, he thought, a kiss or two and possibly more. He hadn't had sex in over a year, the last time an awkward romp with a widow a couple of years older who lived downstairs in his apartment building. With his divorce underway, it seemed more an act of desperation than a triumph, and it left him feeling empty. He'd had enough of love and loss and now felt safer being alone.

The door opened before James could knock.

"Hello," Tara said.

She stood there in a white robe, her hair pulled back in a ponytail, and even without makeup, she was stunning. But she looked sad too, her eyes downcast and her bearing timid, and she might have even shed a couple of pounds since the last time he saw her.

"This is for you," James said.

She took the letter, looked at it, and he searched for any indications of joy or surprise, something to brighten her mood.

"My sister," she said, rubbing her thumb along the envelope, a moment of quiet reflection. "Thank you."

"Jerry said you hadn't come by in a few days."

"I haven't."

The conversation stalled and, for the first time, she seemed less eager to talk than him. As James stood facing her, he felt the warm rush of kinship or sympathy or pity—he wasn't quite sure. He was so removed from the subtleties of human emotions that he sometimes had a hard time distinguishing between them. But he was concerned enough about her to linger, worried enough to ask, "Are you okay?"

Tara stared at the letter again and then looked up, her lips pressed together, her eyes distant.

"As good as can be. Maybe a little under the weather."

He accepted the answer and pushed no further, knowing what it was like to want privacy. It seemed like the right time to go, but he didn't want to leave her in such distress so he kept talking.

"Is there anything I can get?—"

"No, I'm fine," she said.

He looked out to the yard, the trees and the fields beyond, and thought about the dead rabbit on the road, the image still fresh in his mind.

"Have you seen Rod today?" he asked.

"Not today. Why? Has he run off again?"

"No. I mean...I don't know. Just curious."

James waited another minute until the silence became unbearable.

"Let me know if you need anything," he said.

"I will."

With that, he nodded goodbye and started to walk back to the car.

"James," Tara called out, and he turned around.

"Thank you," she said.

Their eyes met and he forced a smile, wondering if she meant it about the letter or something more general.

Thirteen

TARA HAD BEEN ON THE ROAD FOR OVER THREE HOURS AND
had to pee so badly it hurt. But with only twenty miles to go, she was
determined to get to Belleek without stopping, or if she did it would be
at the service station in Cloghore, a building so precariously situated
that its front half was in the Republic and its back in Northern Ireland.

She drove slowly, her hands gripping the wheel, her coat and pocketbook on the seat beside her, along with a map from the Royal Automobile Club. So far, she hadn't needed it, following the motorways across
the west coast of Ireland—through Westport, Castlebar, Ballina, and
Sligo. She and Kevin had used the guide for a similar trip a few months
before he died, and as one of the last items they shared together, she
brought it along as much for sentiment as for direction.

A car passed her on the left and Tara jumped, putting her hand to
her heart. She had been anxious the entire trip and was startled by every
small sound, every abrupt movement. It was ironic that the one time she
needed a valium she couldn't have it, both because she was driving and
because she wanted to be alert for the border guards. She had been
taking the drug as prescribed, on days when she was exceedingly anxious
or depressed, but she didn't like the feeling, and it gave her a drowsy
euphoria that was like the aftereffects of the flu.

When she got off at the exit, she saw the service station but decided she could wait. She continued down the small pastoral lane, hedges on one side and a stone wall on the other, and with Blondie's *The Tide Is High* playing softly on the radio, it felt like a quiet country drive.

Until she came around the next bend.

Immediately, Tara hit the brakes, slowing down behind a traffic backup on the road to Belleek. Up ahead, she could see the ominous bulwarks of the border checkpoint, its corrugated steel walls and camouflage watch tower. British soldiers moved about, leaning into windows and inspecting passports and other forms of ID. The line was about a ¼ mile long, with cars, busses, lorries, tractors—even a horse cart—but it seemed to be moving, and there was an orderly, almost solemn tone to the procession. With prisoners ramping up for another hunger strike, everyone was on edge, civilians and military personnel alike, and the weekend before, the IRA had set off more bombs in Belfast and Derry.

A young soldier walked up to her window, so young, Tara thought, that he looked like a boy. She smiled and handed him her information.

"Good afternoon," he said. "What's your business in Northern Ireland today?"

"Visiting my sister."

"And how long will you be staying?"

"Just the afternoon."

The soldier nodded and then stepped over to a superior, and all at once, she felt her blood pressure rise. She didn't know if this was standard procedure—she didn't know if there even was a procedure. She had only driven to the North a handful of times since Kevin's death, and it was always different, depending on the location and the political situation. Once she had been simply waved through; another time she was asked to step out and her car was searched.

Moments later, the soldier returned and handed her back her documents.

"Carry on, Ms. Evers."

Tara tried to smile but her lips twitched. She put the car in gear, rolled through the gate, and continued down the road where, in the distance, she could see the grand Belleek Pottery building on the far side of the River Erne. She crossed the bridge and entered the small town of Belleek, turning into the hotel that Alice had specified in her letter. Tara would have preferred somewhere more remote, somewhere less obvious, but there wasn't time to write back, and Alice was impossible to reach by phone. Either way, Alice knew more about the risks, living on the front line of the conflict, and for once Tara had to rely on her little sister.

She parked and hurried inside, heading straight down a long hallway to the toilets because she was ready to burst. When she came back out, she went through the lobby and peered into the bar area.

"Gwen?" someone said in a hushed voice.

Hearing her real name gave her a momentary fright until she saw Alice, seated on a black leather couch, a pint on the table in front of her. Tara looked around then walked over, relieved that they were the only two people in there.

Alice had completely changed her hair, darkening it and cropping it short on the front and sides, leaving the back long.

"What did you do?" Tara asked.

"Do ya like it?" Alice asked, turning her head.

"You're gorgeous any which way. It reminds me of Pat Benatar."

"I was thinking more like Joan Jett."

Tara didn't know who that was, but she chuckled anyway and took a seat. A waitress wandered in from the dining room, which was also empty, and she seemed surprised to see another customer. With the tourist season still months away, most hotels were either closed or operating at half-staff, open mainly for winter weddings and other events.

Tara ordered a glass of wine, and the woman went to the bar to get it.

"How's Father?"

"The same really," Alice said. "I didn't tell him we were meeting."

"Afraid he'd be concerned?"

"Afraid he'd wanna tag along."

Tara smiled to herself, always envious of the relationship her sister had with their father.

"And auntie?"

"She's well. She asked about the American."

"He's...interesting—"

The waitress returned with the drink, and they waited until she was gone.

"Sorry for the short notice," Alice said, leaning forward. Her eyes were bloodshot, but for once Tara thought it was from nerves and not because she was high. "There's some news."

"I haven't read anything."

"It's not been in the papers yet." Tara had some of her wine, more than a sip but less than a gulp, and Alice continued. "The trial has been postponed 'til August because of everything that's going on."

Everything that's going on. Tara was amused by the phrase, and she never realized how understated the Irish were until she moved to London, where she was exposed to other cultures from around the world.

"Well, I've waited this long."

"That's not the whole of it," her sister said, a slight dread in her voice. "They've told the judge there's a new witness."

Alice stopped and stared across to her with a serious, almost penetrating look.

"It's not me—" Tara said, defensively.

"Because if—"

"For godsakes, Alice!"

Tara shook her head and turned away, appalled enough that she could have shouted and cried at the same time. She didn't blame her sister, however, and the tension that rose between them was a consequence of things beyond their control. Tara had hoped that by moving to London she could escape The Troubles, and she had always felt guilty about it. Raised in the Bible-steeped world of working-class Belfast, she rejected the vengeful God of her upbringing. But maybe, she thought, this was some kind of punishment, some lesson about the perils of abandoning your own tribe.

After a long silence, Alice had some of her Guinness and mumbled something under her breath that Tara didn't wholly disagree with.

"The bastards deserve it."

The sun was beginning to set as Tara crossed into Galway Country, Killary Fjord opening wide, mountains on both sides stretching to the sea. She was relieved to be out of the North, far from all the political strife, but she was still shaken. Visiting her sister was usually a pleasure, and for the past ten months, Alice had been her only connection to her family. But it also reminded her why she was living out here, a rural exile for a crime she didn't commit. It wasn't enough that she lost her husband, but she had to deal with the aftermath of having loved someone she didn't fully know.

She thought about Kevin the whole ride home, recalling the morning the police came to her flat, two young Bobbies and a detective wearing a tartan vest and bellbottoms like he was going to a disco. What official wears bellbottoms? It was the first thought that came to mind, some petty observation or distraction to delay the awful news she knew was forthcoming.

Or did she know?

For Tara, it had always been more of a hunch than a suspicion—the late nights out, the new friends, the unexplained phone calls, usually whispered and always urgent. She had first bonded with Kevin because they were from the same divided city, never caring that they were on opposite ends of that divide. A Catholic, her father sternly remarked, the first and only time she had taken her new boyfriend over to meet her parents. It was the summer of '73, and tensions between the two communities had reached a boiling point. A month earlier, an IRA bomb had killed five British soldiers in Tyrone, and just a week before six Protestant civilians suffered a similar fate. With society on the verge of a civil war, security was at an all-time high, and Tara and Kevin waited over four hours just to get through customs. It was a trip she would never forget, and for a long time, she never went back. In London, they were just another young couple, foolish and carefree, but back home in Belfast, their differing religious backgrounds was a scandal.

As Tara stood in the doorway that night, draped in Kevin's bathrobe, a coterie of police before her, the only words she heard were "detonated," "instantly," and "unidentifiable." Considering how much of the violence in Northern Ireland spilled over into England, the men were unexpectedly sympathetic. But they needed her to come to head-quarters immediately, which she did, and for the next six hours, she was questioned by Scotland Yard about Kevin and his accomplices. All her life she had been honest to a fault, unlike her sister, who their father said could convince you that the sky was the ocean. And so the agents believed her, and after submitting an affidavit stating she knew nothing about Kevin's involvement in the IRA, she was free to go.

Leaving the station that night was like going from a nightmare to a fever dream. Instead of getting a taxi, Tara walked home from Finsbury to Bayswater in the pouring rain, collapsing on the front steps of her building until an elderly Jamaican neighbor roused her and helped her up to her flat. In the days that followed, the incident was all over the news, photographs of the two dead men and the three who had survived and were now on the run. Tara thought nothing more could upset her until she realized that the picture of Kevin used by the BBC had been taken by police off her nightstand.

The story of *The Mayfair Five* eventually faded, a minor operation in an ancient and ongoing struggle, and because it had been bungled, they wouldn't even be honored for their sacrifices, something Tara was deeply conflicted about. She was never told the intended target of the attack, but she was somewhat reassured in knowing that most IRA bombings were meant to intimidate and not to hurt anyone. Kevin was the gentlest soul she ever met, and although she was sure he had noble reasons for joining, she refused to think of him as a killer.

By the time she turned onto her road, she had thought enough and cried enough for a lifetime, and there was something soothing about being emotionally drained. She pulled into the yard and, for the first time, was glad to be home in Connemara.

She grabbed her things and got out, her legs stiff from driving, and as she approached the door, she saw a cooking pot on the threshold. Underneath it was a note, which she pulled out and began to read.

Tara,

. . .

I made beef stew tonight and thought you might want some.

James

The gesture was heartwarming, as was the letter, and she couldn't help but observe that he wrote how he spoke, simply and with no elaboration. After the day she just had, the gift meant more than a string of pearls, and she was, in fact, hungry. Tara smiled to herself and looked down towards the cottage, where she saw a light on in the kitchen, the smoke of burning turf rising from the old chimney.

After living alone on the peninsula all winter, the arrival of a stranger from America had given her some hope for companionship, and maybe she had been overeager. She had expected too much and James let her down, and now that she expected nothing, he surprised her. Wasn't that always the way, she thought, the mysterious spontaneity of human goodwill which, much like the tide, was steady but unpredictable.

Tara realized then that she had tried to understand James without knowing him, more concerned with where he came from than where he was going. They were both broken souls, that was obvious, but how could she ever expect him to open up when she herself was living a life of secrets and half-truths?

Fourteen

❧

JAMES STOOD AGAINST THE LADDER ON THE SIDE OF THE
house, three nails in his mouth and a hammer in hand. The old gutter,
clogged with dead leaves and other detritus of the wind, had pulled away
from the eaves and leaked whenever it rained, staining the plaster wall
with the resins of its putrefied vegetation. He raised it up a few inches
and held it in place, balancing precariously while he reached for a nail
and positioned it. He tapped it into the grains until it was steady and
then swung the hammer.

"Dammit!"

The nail bent, splintering the wood and going in at an angle. This
was a job for two men, James thought, as he spit another nail into his
hand. He had been in construction long enough to know, his years
watching cut-rate builders who were understaffed or who didn't have all
the right tools. If his father had taught him and his brother anything, it
was the honor of the work, and there was nothing more insulting to a
house than altering it ill-equipped.

He drove another nail, which also went at a slight angle but caught
the house. The last was the coup de grâce, a perfect shot through the
wood and into the fascia, securing the gutter to the eaves.

James hooked the hammer on his belt, went down the ladder, and got a headrush as he touched the ground. He was irritable and unfocused, which he saw as no excuse for his sloppy work. He had finally gotten a letter from his lawyer, who wrote to inform him that, per his request, the case against his brother had been dismissed without prejudice. After years of litigation, the false starts and dashed hopes, the ordeal was finally over. His attorney had advised him against it, of course, insisting that his brother had unlawfully assumed ownership and control over the family business and that James had every right to sue. But James was tired of wanting for things which, in the end, didn't seem to want him, and so he let go of his brother the same way he let go of his ex-wife, with a quiet and bitter civility.

He expected more relief after getting the letter but instead felt a numb acceptance like he never really had a choice. And he preferred to see it that way because throughout his life, whenever he tried to exert his will upon the world it backfired. The only time his temper and rage were of any use was in the war, an experience which, despite all the pain and horror, was something he often missed.

James reached into his shirt pocket for his cigarettes and walked over to the garden, where two weathered chairs lay half-submerged in the moss. As he sat, he wondered if they had been there in his grandmother's time. He looked at the flowerbeds, rebuilt with the help of the local boys, and saw the tiny buds of crocuses sprouting in the soil. In the cold harshness of these endless days, it was hard to imagine there would ever be a spring.

Rod came over, drowsy like he had just woken up, his tail down. As James reached to pat him under the scruff, he heard a soft voice.

"Hello."

He glanced over his shoulder, and Tara was standing on the lawn. He blew smoke out his nose but didn't say anything.

"I just wanted to stop by and say thanks," she said.

She started walking towards him across the yard.

"Thanks?" he muttered.

"For the stew."

"Oh, right."

"Mind if I sit?"

He flicked an ash, cleared his throat.

"Be my guest."

The chair creaked as she sat, and when she crossed her legs, James worried it might collapse. He didn't look over, although he was glad for the company, and for the next few minutes, they sat in the windless silence of the gray afternoon.

"So quiet," Tara said, finally.

"Isn't it always."

"I guess it is. But they say a big storm's coming in."

"That so."

"I heard it on the radio."

Rod got up and went over, rubbing against her leg and looking for affection.

"James," Tara said, and he cringed. In her voice, he heard the same wavering emotion his ex-wife used to have when she had something important to say. "I wanted to apologize for last weekend."

James curled his lips and looked down at his hands, which were dry and chapped.

"I should have said it the other evening when you came by," she added. "I just wasn't...feeling up to it."

"You didn't seem right."

"I wasn't. I had to drive up to the North the next morning. It always puts me in a foul mood."

He accepted the excuse with a long nod, although he didn't entirely believe it. He could tell something was wrong the night he took the mail over, her vacant stare and glassy eyes more than too much wine and too little sleep could produce. He had lived long enough, had been in enough tough spots, to read people, and he trusted his instincts. James didn't believe Tara was lying outright, but she wasn't telling him everything, and it made him suspicious.

"It's hard to go home," was all he said.

Hearing the crunch of feet, they both looked over and the three boys from across the hill were coming into the yard, dressed in their uniforms, schoolbags hanging from their shoulders. James flicked his cigarette and got up, and Tara did the same.

"You ready to work?" he asked.

They nodded in unison, and he looked over to the side of the cottage.

"I fixed the downspout. We've gotta dig a trench for the rainwater."

Tara smiled and turned to him.

"I'm going into the village," she said. "Need anything?"

He thought for a moment, and it wasn't about her question. Not having eaten all day, his mouth began to water, and although he had the urge to spit, he refrained for her sake.

"Naw," he said. "But thanks anyway."

Tara stepped around him, waving with a cute smile. He watched as she walked away, tiptoeing in her leather boots, her figure swaying like beach grass. James didn't feel ashamed for staring because his concern was more about her psyche than her sex appeal. Since the day they met, she was always polite and put together, her blouses ironed and her makeup just right. But behind those dark eyes, he could sense a deeper anguish, like a muted scream that was trying to get out. The struggle in her was the struggle in him and, for the first time, he got the urge to protect her however he could.

"Sir?"

James startled and turned to see the oldest boy.

"We need another shovel, sir," he said.

Distracted, James rubbed his chin, catching the last sight of Tara before she disappeared around the hedges.

"Um, there's a spade behind the back wall."

Tara walked into Joyce's and was glad to see only a couple of men at the bar. It seemed that every time she shopped, she had to endure some unsolicited question, comment, or remark, the hapless flirtations of locals and laborers, pensioners and drunks. Sometimes it was amusing, but more often than not it was annoying, and she saw their badgering as the residual chauvinism of the days when women weren't allowed in. If there was any sign of how far rural society had come with gender equality, she thought, it was that the grocer and the pub were now combined.

She waited quietly by the register, clutching her pocketbook and avoiding eye contact. Behind the counter, she saw the shelf of sweets: Crunchie's and Curly Wurly's, Fun Gums and Cadbury Flake's. There was a bucket of penny chews too, Blackjacks, Fruit Salads, Mojos, and more. She thought back warmly to their family's shop, the afternoons spent refilling jars, she and her sister dressed in their red and blue school outfits. Whenever their father stepped out, they would stuff their mouths and their pockets, giggling all the while until he returned and pretended not to know. Those were the days of lost innocence, long before the riots and unrest, and although Tara couldn't have known it then, it was the happiest time of her life.

"Miss?"

She turned and saw Jerry, who was trying to open the door while holding a two-wheeled dolly. She looked over to the bar patrons, who seemed unaware, and then ran to help.

"Lovely, thanks," he said.

The boxes were piled to the top, stamped with the name of a wholesale butcher in Galway City.

"That's enough meat to feed an army," Tara said.

"We need to stock up before the storm."

He rolled the dolly across the floor and set it beside the counter, wiping his forehead and then looking up.

"Now," Jerry said. "What can I get ye?"

"Do you have candles?"

"Taper or pillar?"

"Pillar, please," she said. "Five or so. And a side of ham, quart of milk."

When Jerry walked out back, Tara glanced discreetly towards the bar. The television was on, as it always was, and although the volume was low, a news story caught her attention and she froze. Images of the three men who had survived the explosion that killed Kevin flashed across the screen, and she knew it was about the postponement of the trial. Because it happened in a flat in Mayfair, the media had dubbed them *The Mayfair Five*, the fleeting celebrity of a group of young men who would only be remembered for a botched bombing.

As she watched, she was seized by a quiet dread, breathing rapidly and at the edge of tears. At that moment, she would have swallowed a valium dry, but she'd left them at home and so had to face the private terror unsoothed. The segment was over in twenty seconds, moving on to more important stories like Margaret Thatcher's visit to the U.S. and Prince Charles's engagement to Lady Diana Spencer. Still, it left her shaken, sick with fear but also sadness.

"You okay, Miss?"

Tara turned and Jerry was waiting at the counter.

"Oh, yes. Sorry."

"What *is* your name?" he said. "You've been coming in for ages now."

"Right. It's...Tara."

"Well, Tara, these aren't pretty..." He held up a fat, yellow candle. "But they'll do the job if you lose power."

"I might be under water by then."

"You've got quite a neighbor to protect you."

She looked up, her mouth agape.

"How do you mean?"

"The American," Jerry said. "I'm told he's a war hero."

"I wouldn't know anything about that."

He put everything in a bag and rang it in.

"Anything else?"

"Um," she said, looking past him to the candy. "A bag of Milky Mints, please."

He put them on the counter, and Tara reached in her purse, searching for the right change, her fingers trembling uncontrollably. She didn't glance up to see if he noticed, but she got self-conscious nonetheless, and when someone at the bar called for a drink, it only added to the pressure.

"Take your time," Jerry said gently.

Finally, she got it together, three Irish pounds and a handful of tens and twenty-cent coins. She dropped it all in his hand, took the bag, and turned around and left. She was embarrassed that she didn't say thank you or goodbye, but she didn't have a choice, overcome by a claustrophobic dread that left her dizzy and gasping for air. A *panic attack* her sister called it, one of the few times Tara ever confided in someone else about her periodic fits of despondency. She had one or two as a young adult, but they mostly started after Kevin's death.

Once outside, she breathed in the cold, damp air and began to feel better. As she approached her car, her eyes caught a yellow license plate a few vehicles away and she stopped. She had never seen a car from Northern Ireland in the area, even during the tourist season. Frightened, she backed away and ducked into a driveway, coming out to a small clearing behind the shops that was bordered by a stone wall, the pastures and hills beyond.

Suddenly, someone called her name and Tara gasped. She walked fast, glancing back every few steps, her heart pounding. After months of hiding, the worst had come true, she thought, but if they had finally come for her, she wasn't going to die in an alley.

She ran to the end of the row of buildings and headed back towards the main street, clutching her groceries and resigned to any outcome. When she came around the corner, a man stood waiting for her on the sidewalk.

"Jerry?" she said.

"You forgot your Milky Mints."

Fifteen

WHEN TARA WOKE UP, SHE LOOKED AT THE CLOCK AND IT was almost 10 a.m. In the past couple of weeks, she had been sleeping in later and later, which was either a sign of her improvement or her further decline. The truth was she couldn't tell because she spent most of her time alone, and it was impossible to assess her own condition. Although the drugs made her woozy in the day, they had been helping her sleep at night, and she was no longer restless.

She got up and went in the shower, rubbing the soap between her hands, struggling to make suds in the dry, morning air. She got dressed and headed to the kitchen, where she turned on the kettle and got a scone from the cabinet. She sat at the table by the window, eating with no appetite, still reeling from the incident in the village the day before.

She knew she had overreacted, the latent paranoia of her months in seclusion, but it also reminded her that she was still at risk. Her long-term hope, the one her sister and other family members shared, was that the trial proceeded quietly, that the suspects be given their due process, and that the whole horrible affair would come to an end.

Tara had known nothing about Kevin's activities, and even the investigators cleared her as a possible accomplice or witness. But her part was significant enough that, shortly after his death, someone contacted

Alice's boyfriend and suggested that she 'disappear' for a while. Her sister never said who it was, but Tara was sure that, like most men who worked at the shipyards, Walter had connections with Protestant para-militaries, and they always watched out for members of their own community. At the time, she was too distraught to be grateful for the advice, but at the urging of her father and her sister, she took it and was gone the next morning.

After ten months of exile, Tara would have expected the danger to be over. But *The Mayfair Five* were now back in the news, the trial delayed because of the worsening political situation in the North. And if the prosecution had also named a new witness, like Alice claimed, then it might make the IRA suspicious enough to finally come looking for her.

She put on her coat, grabbed her hat and gloves, and went out. The sky was a deep gray, the wind gentle, and as she walked down the road, she could tell the tide was in because it didn't smell. Tara never thought of herself as a country girl, having spent most of her life in two of the biggest cities in the UK, but she was starting to feel more at home among the wildness of nature, sensing patterns in things that once seemed random, the cry of the thrush at dawn, the shifting of the winds each afternoon, the tender call-and-response of sheep and their offspring.

As she passed the cottage, she was surprised that James wasn't in the yard. Soon he would run out of things to repair, she thought, and if he started to makeover the kitchen or shingle the roof, she would have to stop him there. She understood the sentiment which drove him, but it wasn't his house and it wasn't hers, and although she knew it was unlikely, she didn't want her aunt to be in the awkward position of defending her property against a squatter's claim. Nevertheless, Tara admired James' diligence and the daily purpose it provided, somedays wishing that she too had a pastime or hobby to keep her busy.

She came to the end of the road and followed the narrow trail between the rocks. In the distance, a small fishing boat was floating just offshore, and when she came out on the beach, she saw the three school-boys. They stood in a row, tugging a long rope that ended at their uncle's vessel, and as Tara got closer, she noticed a pile of tangled gill nets, dripping wet and covered in dark algae.

"Afternoon, Miss," one of them called out.

"Done for the day?"

"Hauling it in for the storm."

She smiled and continued on, the cold water sheeting over the sand only inches from her feet. So far, she had lived through a dozen coastal squalls, the wind and rain often so intense that they seemed to shake the foundations of the earth. Even in the safety of her house, built of stone block and mortar, she sometimes worried she would get swept out to sea. She never slept during storms, waiting out the hours like she did her lonely solitude, with a long and patient angst.

Startled by a noise, Tara looked ahead and Rod burst from the tall grass, his tongue out and tail fluttering. He scurried over and began to circle her, as restless as a newborn colt.

"He seems to like you."

When she turned, James was at the top of the bluff, a stick in hand and a subtle grin on his face.

"This is quite a welcome," she said, reaching down to pat Rod.

James came down the rocks and made his way towards her. With no hat, his hair flowed freely in the breeze, and she was surprised how long it had gotten. His face was nearly as dark as his beard, the result of working outdoors, and she envied his winter tan.

"Sounds like this storm might be something big," she said.

"Sure does."

He flung the stick, and Rod ran after it. When James started to walk, she walked with him, and he didn't seem to mind. Each time the dog brought back the stick, James would throw it again, over and over, a game which seemed, for both of them, a source of infinite entertainment.

At the end of the beach, they came to a rocky inlet that was shaped like a bowl. With the tide at its peak, ocean water heaved in and out of it, thrashing and churning in a haze of white foam that left just enough clarity to see the bottom.

They stopped and Rod continued around the edge of the formation, sniffing at kelp and other debris, at times spooked by a sudden rush of seaspray.

"When I was a boy," James said, "I used to swim here with my cousins."

Tara turned, looked up to him.

"Wouldn't the barnacles hurt your feet?"

"Sometimes," he said. "But it was worth it."

They headed away from the water and towards the dry ground of the bluff, Rod following but also keeping his distance.

"Are you close with your cousins?"

"Not in years," James said, shaking his head. "After my father died, we all lost touch."

"Surely you could look them up?"

"One lives in Australia. The other is a sailor, so God knows where he could be."

With a wistful laugh, he glanced at her, and Tara filled with a warm elation. She had learned more about him in the past five minutes than in the previous five weeks, and sometimes the simplest conversations revealed the most. She wanted to know more, of course, but she wouldn't pry, and she was content enough to chat and have a little companionship.

They started up a shallow hill, where the grass along the shore turned to bogland and pastures, and soon the surf was replaced by the sounds of cows and sheep. They stepped through a break in a wall and came into a field that was empty and overgrown. In one corner was a stone structure, the remnants of a Famine home, a poignant reminder of Ireland's distant but devastating past.

James hurled the stick, sending it to the far side of the clearing, and Rod took off. Suddenly, there was a loud bark, and Tara saw another dog come out from the weeds. It was much larger than Rod, with a thick, dark coat, and it moved with the stealth of a wolf.

"He looks feral," James said.

He hurried towards them and Tara followed.

"Quick!" she said. "Call him back!"

He tried, but Rod stood frozen, tail raised and facing his opponent with a slow and simmering growl. Tara could tell he was scared, but his instincts instructed him to stand his ground, the destructive pride of nature.

Just as they got close, the big dog lunged and went straight at Rod, tackling him to the ground. Tara screamed and James ran over and tried to use his boot to separate them. But the animals fought on ferociously, rolling through the grass in a whirlwind of paw swipes and snapping jaws. Handicapped by his age and size, Rod held his own at first, but soon the wild dog overwhelmed him, and Tara watched in horror as Rod flailed, his snout scratched and bloody.

"Sunofabitch!"

James shouted with such violent rage that it seemed to echo across the valley. In a calm, almost methodical manner, he walked over and got on top of the animal, who now had Rod pinned and was preparing for the kill. Sensing someone behind it, the dog turned back and tried to unleash its fury on James. But it didn't get more than one or two nips before James grabbed it in a bear hug. Then with a quick, powerful jerk, he broke its neck.

Tara cringed and looked away. When she turned back, she watched as the animal fell to the side and landed with a thump—dead. James lifted up Rod, who whimpered like a child in his arms, and said, "I gotta get him home."

"Sir!"

They looked and the three boys from the beach were running towards them, probably drawn by the commotion.

"That your dog?" James said, nodding to the carcass in the grass.

They all shook their heads, wide-eyed and amazed that the animal had been slain.

"It's wild, sir. Our Da thinks it's been killing the lambs."

"Are there a lot of wild dogs out here?"

They shrugged their shoulders, looked at each other.

"Not like in packs, sir," the tall boy said. "Sometimes if an old farmer dies, his dogs will go free."

"You killed it!" the youngest one said.

When Tara looked at James, he averted his eyes, his forehead damp from exertion.

"Naw," he said. "That animal killed itself."

~

James was still rattled as he and Tara came up the road from the shore. He had carried Rod much of the way, but at some point, he realized the dog was only exploiting his sympathy so he put him down and made him walk. James had learned that you always give someone the least assistance necessary, otherwise you would make them dependent. Besides, he was wounded too. Tara was the first to notice the bitemarks on his coat, so strong they had punctured the thick, wool fabric. He could feel soreness, and even some swelling, but he wouldn't know if the skin was broken until he got home and undressed.

James respected the wild dog for fighting back, and it was always harder to kill something that didn't resist. But as the adrenaline wore off, his rage was replaced by a vague sympathy because he saw the animal as a victim too. If the war had taught him anything, it was that there was no such thing as blind hatred and that all living things acted only in the interest of their own survival. The way he felt about the dog was the same way he felt about dead Viet Cong soldiers, that strange comradery among enemies. But it wasn't a pity that forgave or gave in. James didn't love much in this world, but Rod was the closest thing to a friend or family he had, and the animal that attacked him had no better chance of living than if it had gone after a lion's cub.

When they reached the cottage, they stopped and turned to each other. James was just about to say goodbye when Tara blurted, "Why don't you come up to the house. I'll take a look at that bite."

He hesitated for a second, then decided to accept, and it was more out of necessity because he didn't have gauze or clean bandages.

"Sure," he said.

They continued up the road, Rod limping close behind, and walked into the yard. Tara opened the front door, giving the dog a skeptical look before waving him in too. James knew she didn't like having animals in the house, and what woman would? She must have realized by now that he didn't go anywhere without Rod, and he appreciated her quiet tolerance.

Inside, the house smelled of lilacs or lilies—James could never distinguish between flowers—but when he looked around and didn't see a vase, he assumed it was incense, or maybe her perfume. A home always smelled different when a woman occupied it, something he discovered after he and his wife separated and he had to get an apartment.

"Have a seat," Tara said, going over to the kitchen. "How about some tea?"

"Sounds good."

James sat on the couch, and Rod wandered around the parlor, sniffing at things and looking for a good place to lie down.

"How's your arm?" she asked.

"I think fine."

She put on the kettle and walked over to the fireplace. As she knelt down to stack some turf, her shirt and sweater rose up, revealing the small of her back and the deep curves of her waist. James was captivated by the sight of her smooth, white skin, and as unseemly as it was, he couldn't stop staring until she glanced back and he quickly turned away.

"I thought you were crazy today," she said.

"Pardon?"

The kettle whistled, and she went over to get it.

"When you jumped on that dog," she said. "I thought you were crazy to do it."

"I didn't really have a choice."

She spooned loose tea from a can, and he wondered why the Irish used leaves instead of bags. She poured the hot water and came over, handing him a cup and sitting down.

"You frightened the hell out of me," Tara said.

He thought it was an accusation until she gave a cute smile as she brought the drink to her lips.

"I would have warned you. It just happened so fast."

She was as close to him as the night she was drunk and came onto him. But for some reason, he didn't have the same reluctance and was unexpectedly comfortable in her presence.

"Do you feel bad about it?" she asked.

James raised his eyebrows, surprised by the question.

"He was gonna hurt my dog," he said. "Besides, that mutt's been raising hell. You heard what those boys said."

Tara nodded as if the explanation somehow satisfied her conscience. "Let's see that bite," she said.

He put his tea down on the table and removed his jacket. When he held out his arm, she took it in both hands, and he felt a faint tingle, the onset of goosebumps. She pulled up the sleeve of his dark flannel shirt, and he could see tiny red marks on his forearm, traces of dried blood around them.

"He got you pretty good. Wait here."

She got up and went down the hallway, returning moments later with a box of Band-Aids, some rubbing alcohol, and a face towel.

"Take off your shirt," she said.

It seemed unnecessary, but James didn't hesitate because he didn't want to seem shy or embarrassed. He undid the buttons and pulled off his shirt, the cool air giving him a slight chill. Tara poured some rubbing alcohol on the towel and pressed it against the wounds. At first, it stung, but he didn't flinch, and he watched as she ran it up and down his forearm in long, soothing strokes. She peered up every few seconds, her lashes fluttering, and her touch was so sensual that he was soon aroused.

"Does that hurt?" she asked.

He shook his head and leaned back into the couch. She opened a bandage and put it over one of the bitemarks.

"Keep these covered," she said softly.

"I'll try."

She took out another one and applied it.

"There's no rabies in Ireland."

"So, I've heard."

"But that doesn't mean it can't get infected."

Tara worked her way down his arm, covering each wound with the delicacy of a surgeon. She opened the last Band-Aid, struggling with the wrapper, and it fell between his legs. As she reached for it, her hand rubbed against his thigh and he tensed up. He looked at her and she was staring back. Whether it was an accident or intentional, he really didn't know, but this time he wasn't going to let her make the first move.

With their eyes locked, James came towards her, and she didn't retreat or resist. He brought his lips to hers and they kissed. At first, it was light, but then she opened her mouth and it became something deeper and more intense. When Tara put her hands on his chest, he started to undo her blouse, proceeding against all his better instincts. In coming to Ireland, he had sworn off humanity and all the disappointments of love and life. But in the throes of passion, there was no time to reassess so when she fell back onto the couch, he followed her. And as they frantically pulled off each other's clothing, he felt sad for the both of them, knowing there could never be a future.

When Tara walked out in her robe, James was kneeling by the fireplace, Rod curled up on the rug next to him. At some point during the night, they had moved into the bedroom, lying close but facing away from each other. While he was out cold, she couldn't sleep but she didn't toss for fear of waking him. His slow, steady breathing reminded her of Kevin and, at times, she even got a tinge of guilt. But Kevin was never the jealous kind, and she knew he would have wanted her to find someone else.

She watched as he stirred the coals, his boots untied and his shirt hung loose enough that she could see the scars under his ribcage that she had noticed the night before.

"Mornin'," he said, startling her by looking up.

"Good morning."

"I made you some tea, in the pot."

"Thanks."

As Tara walked over to the kitchen, she felt a soreness that she hadn't had in a long time. She smiled to herself, thinking back to the night she lost her virginity at a party at the Queen's Student's Union in her last year of college. At the time, tensions were starting to flare across Northern Ireland—there had been rioting in Derry, more sectarian assassinations—and with the future uncertain, everyone lived a little recklessly. The fact that Tara forgot the boy's name but remembered he was a Catholic was significant, and her friends joked that her doing it was a sacrifice in the name of religious unity.

She poured a cup and walked over, looking down at Rod.

"He loves the warmth."

"Well," James said, standing up. "He probably went a long time without it."

As he faced her, she got a sudden urge for more sex and was glad it went away because it was never good to be too willing. She didn't sleep with Kevin until they were together three months—a long courtship even back then—and when you were young there was dignity in waiting. But Tara was older now, long past dreams of making a family or building a legacy, and the intimacy she sought now was as much for pleasure as it was for emotional survival.

"I gotta get back," he said.

As he reached for his coat, she wondered what he had to *get back* to —everyone out here had a routine to help them through the long days.

"I had fun last night," she said.

"Me too."

Their words were short, disjointed.

"Thanks."

"Well—"

"I'll see you—"

"Of course—"

Finally, they both laughed, breaking the awkwardness of the moment. As she walked him to the door, Tara waited to see if he would kiss her, and she wasn't let down when he didn't because she knew there would be other times.

Sixteen

JAMES DIDN'T KNOW HOW TO PREPARE FOR A STORM IN Ireland. In Boston, it was almost a ritual, closing all the windows and stocking up on bread, milk, and butter. If snow was coming, people got their shovels out and lined them up on the porch, and anyone fortunate enough to own a thrower would get fresh gasoline and test start the motor. Not in his neighborhood, however, where most families didn't even have a car. Kids wore plastic bread bags over their boots to keep them dry; they dressed in the mismatched winter clothes they inherited from older siblings. When James was young, they lived in a third-floor apartment that still used coal heat, and he and his brother would help their father scoop it through the basement window into a bin. He always saw storms as hard work, but they also brought about a wondrous anticipation, the thrill and fury of nature and that agonizing uncertainty over whether or not there would be school the next morning.

Unlike American cities, the coast of Connemara, with its bald hills and rugged vegetation, seemed built for bad weather. The homes were all made of concrete block, so sturdy they were like extensions of the rocky landscape, and James had seen the cottage withstand gusts that would have torn off a roof back home. Because it rarely snowed in

Ireland, no one worried about how the roads would be cleared, and trees were so few and scattered that they posed no real risk to the power lines. With the village a few miles away, food was never easy to get anyway, and the entire region seemed steeped in self-sufficiency.

Considering all this, there was nothing to do but wait, and yet James couldn't sit still. He had already put the ladder, shovel, and tools behind the cottage, securing them with some old rope he found under the sink. He thought about going out to get more supplies, but the day before he had filled his tank, got 40 lbs. of turf and several boxes of fire starters. He bought the last carton of Lucky Strikes at Joyce's and had to settle for a second one of generics. He also got some frozen hamburgers, apples, and potato chips, but he didn't worry about food and had been surviving mainly off cigarettes and coffee anyway.

James knew he wouldn't freeze or starve to death, but he wasn't sure he could stay sane. He paced the room with his coffee, peering through the shades like he was waiting for an attack. The sea was still calm, but the horizon was a wall of gray tumult, slowly overtaking the sky, creeping towards the coast.

Snuggled by the fire, Rod looked up every few minutes as if he could sense his master's unease. And his instincts were right because James was irritable to the core, a feeling he both hated and thrived on. Of all the contradictions of his life, this was the worst, the addictive bliss of anger, outrage, suspicion. He felt like he had lived his whole life with his fists raised, ready for a fight and consumed by the illusion that if he could just act first then nothing could ever harm him. When taunted in the schoolyard as a boy, he wouldn't hesitate to throw the first punch, and his mother said he had the temper of a mad bull.

His brother was always the more responsible one, hanging up his shirts at night, collecting pennies in a jar which he kept under the bed. He never gave his parents any trouble, unlike James, who ended up enlisting in the Marines after an assault on a subcontractor left him facing a few months in jail and a hefty fine. It was time to grow up, his father said when they parted at South Station, and for the entire train ride to Parris Island, James wondered if he had made the right decision. The mistakes he made as a young man haunted him still, but they also made it easier to believe that, maybe, his brother deserved the business.

Outside, the wind howled. James peered through the window and the yard was dark. Alone in the remote cottage, stuck with only his memories, he saw the storm as some great conclusion to his life. But he wasn't ready quite yet, and he had one final letter to send. Drinking the last of his coffee, he sat at the couch, slid in a piece of paper, and began to type.

Dear Mrs. Rodriguez,

This letter may come as a surprise to you and I am sorry I have not written it until now. I was the commanding officer of your son Joel's platoon when he joined our battalion in the summer of '67. At the time, we were stationed at the U.S. airbase in Danang and with nothing to do but sit and wait, we all got to know each other well. The men very much liked and respected Joel. Being from Boston, I really enjoyed hearing his stories about growing up in Del Rio, Texas. I remember him telling me how you once found him sleeping with a scorpion in his crib, but you didn't wake him because you were afraid he would startle it and get stung. The stories we all shared about our lives made us feel a little closer to home and the people we loved...

A gust rattled all the windows. James looked over to Rod and was surprised to see the dog staring back.

...In September of that year, our battalion got orders to move north to a small outpost between Con Thien and Gio Linh. Going from the relative safety of Danang to the DMZ was a big shock for all of us. The North Vietnamese had been attacking the base all winter and the previous unit suffered many casualties. It happened mostly after dark so platoons were assigned to guard the perimeter on a rotating basis. I spent many hours in a sandbag lookout with Joel and the other men and our jokes and stories helped us get through those long nights...

. . .

Suddenly, the lights flickered.

...Once we were "seasoned" by a few weeks of duty, command ordered us to do daily reconnaissance missions to keep the enemy on their toes. We would march a couple miles in a wide circle, mostly over low hills and scrubland, and return to base before sundown. By then, Joel had been promoted to sergeant after his predecessor was bitten by a snake and had to be evacuated (he later died).

In early March, we were out on patrol in heavy rain and came under fire. We didn't realize it at the time but we had stumbled upon a North Vietnamese Battalion and we were severely outnumbered. We radioed back to headquarters and were told to try to hold them off until help arrived.

When one of our advance units said the NVA was trying to outflank us along a narrow ridge, I ordered Joel to take his squad and head them off. They left the safety of cover for only a few seconds and were hit by machinegun fire from an enemy position we weren't aware of. Joel and another soldier were badly wounded.

The unit was pinned down for several hours and reinforcements still hadn't arrived. Worried that the men were losing too much blood, I ordered cover fire and ran across an open field to help extract them. For that, I was awarded the Medal of Honor.

When the choppers finally arrived, Joel and the other soldier were evacuated and it was several days later that I found out that Joel had died. For years I have struggled with his death and the order I gave that led to it. When I returned from the war, I did whatever I could to forget the horrible things I experienced there. But I have come to see that pushing it all down only made it worse and I can no longer live...

Boom!

James jumped up from the couch, and Rod barked. He circled the room in a frenzy, his eyes wide and heart pounding, so stunned it took him a moment to realize that the door had blown in. He ran over and held it shut, and when he saw a piece of rusted metal on the floor, he just shook his head. With all the improvements he made, he had forgotten to fix the loose strike plate, and it got torn away from the rotted frame.

He knew he could remount the screws, but he didn't have a screwdriver. He waited for a lull in the weather then got his coat, checking first to make sure he had his pocket flashlight. He grabbed a few sheets of typewriter paper off the table, folding them over and over to create a wedge.

"Stay here, boy," he said, and Rod stood attentive in the middle of the room.

Stepping out, James jammed the paper in the door and pulled it tight. He threw his hood over his head and ran out into the storm.

Tara sat on the couch, dressed in her robe and slippers, a glass in hand. She finished her last bottle of red wine the night James was over, and all she had now was white, which sometimes made her dizzy. She often wished she liked Guinness or other stouts like her sister Alice, but beer tasted bitter, and it always made her feel bloated. In college, her friends would make fun of her, especially the Catholic girls, who said wine was posh, the choice of princes and dukes. Considering it was also part of the sacrament of communion, one of the few things their religions had in common, Tara found the criticism ironic.

Turf smoldered in the fireplace with tiny pops and crackles—two fat candles burned on the table, more for the atmosphere than the smell. Outside the winds were starting to pick up, and when Tara looked through the curtains, leaves, nettles, and other debris were whirling in the air. By now it was dark, and she couldn't see much past the cottage, where the light shone faintly through the side window.

As she stared out, Tara wondered what James was doing. It had been almost a week since they had sex, and she'd only seen him once since, the next morning when he came by with a box of store-bought cakes and some advice about hosing the mud off her car rims so the brakes didn't wear out. When she asked him in for tea, it was the first time he ever answered without hesitation, and for the next hour, they sat at the kitchen table and talked about small things, a conversation that was simple yet intimate.

It was easier that way, Tara thought, getting to know someone by what they didn't say rather than by what they did. Of course, she was curious about his life, if not from some girlish romantic yearning, then at least out of genuine human interest. She didn't know what would come of their relationship—or if anything would—but she accepted that he wasn't a man who could be pressed, tricked, or cajoled into opening up.

As Tara sat thinking, she noticed a small light coming up the road, and the only reason she didn't panic was because it was from the direction of the shore. Moments later, it pierced the hedgerows, and when someone turned into the yard, she knew it was James because by now she recognized his walk.

She put down her glass and hurried over to get the door.

"James?"

"Do you have a screwdriver?"

"I...I think so," she said, wincing at the odd request. "C'mon in."

She went over and got a handyman's box out of the cabinet.

"What could possibly need fixing at this hour?" she asked, opening it.

"The door lock came loose."

"How is it out there?"

"Windy."

Thunder cracked, and they both jumped. Then it started to pour, not the gradual onset of a weekday shower, but thick, violent sheets of rain that sounded like they could break the glass. Tara continued looking, her hand buried under small wrenches, vice grips, screws, tap nails, tangled wire—all the accoutrements of do-it-yourself home maintenance. When she finally felt the steel shank of a screwdriver, she pulled it out of the heap and held it up.

"Will this do?"

"Unfortunately, I need a flathead," he said.

She tried searching some more but had already reached the bottom.

"There might be one in the shed out back. Can it wait?"

He shrugged his shoulders, standing at the door like a deliveryman waiting to get paid so he could leave. Knowing he wasn't shy, she assumed he was aggravated, and a storm was no time to be doing house repairs.

Tara put the box away and came over.

"Won't you stay a while?"

"I really gotta get back," James said. "Rod's alone."

"He won't mind," she said, peering up. "Stay until the rain dies down."

She had never been a good flirt, and as a young woman, her attempts at romance were usually clumsy, facilitated by alcohol and no less sloppy. But she was old enough to understand the ritual of seduction, and when she noticed his eyes sweep past her cleavage, she did nothing to cover up.

"Sure—"

The moment he spoke, thunder roared overhead and instantly, the power went out. They faced each other in the silence of the semi-darkness, shadows from the candlelight flickering on the walls. As a girl, Tara was always spooked by the night and the imagined possibilities of what lurked. Since Kevin's death, that fright had returned, only this time it wasn't for ghosts and banshees but the very real threat that someone was coming to get her. Having James nearby lessened those fears—having him with her made them go away.

Suddenly, she felt a hand on her breast, another on her shoulder. James stepped forward, and when she looked up, he brought his lips to hers. As they kissed, she reached down and undid the knot on her robe, revealing that she was wearing nothing underneath. He took her gently in both arms, pulled her close and she gasped. They drifted towards the couch, almost knocking over the coatrack, and his pants and shirt were off before they got there. She motioned for him to sit, then got on top, riding him endlessly while the storm raged outside.

"What did they do to you?" Tara asked.

When James opened his eyes, she was snuggled behind him and

running her finger along the scars under his arm. Her touch was just like his ex-wife's, he thought, or maybe all women's hands felt the same.

"What?"

"In the War," she said softly. "What happened?"

He gripped the pillow and stared at the wall.

"A situation," he said, as vague as he could be without ignoring the question.

"Why is everyone saying you're a hero?"

James felt his entire body go tense. He rolled over in the bed, his leg tangled in the sheets, and looked at her.

"Who said that?"

"People in the village."

"That's nonsense."

He rolled back but could no longer relax, and each time she tried to get close, he moved away. But he could only go so far, and when he finally reached the edge of the mattress, he jumped out of the bed.

"What's wrong?" she asked.

"I gotta use the bathroom."

He felt around for his jeans and got his penlight. He walked out of the bedroom, down the small hallway, and into the bathroom. Because he couldn't point the light and pee at the same time, he proceeded in darkness, his eyes closed. His breathing was shallow, his mind uneasy. He was anxious, but he wasn't altogether angry, and he didn't blame Tara for her questions. James believed enough in honor to accept that once you slept with a woman, you were no longer the sole guardian of your secrets. But honesty was a two-way street, and something in his gut said that she wasn't telling him everything about herself.

He flushed the toilet and stepped over to the sink, where he turned on the flashlight to find the faucet. As he did, he noticed an unzipped makeup bag on the shelf, stuffed with lipstick cases and mascara, tweezers and other beauty implements. There were pills too, a box of Paracetamol and some generic vitamins. James was never one to snoop, but when the light happened to hit it, he noticed a bottle of valium. He detested drugs, the scourge of the infantry, and had watched many of his good buddies return from Vietnam addicted to heroin and other opiates, surviving a war only to die from the lonely desolation of a junkie. He had no reason to believe Tara was dependent, but the fact that she even needed narcotics said something about her condition. He didn't have time to ponder it, however, because he was more shocked by the name on the label: Gwendolyn M. Evers.

James felt all the blood leave his face. Considering the parallels between love and war, it was like trying to sneak up on the enemy, only to have him ambush you from behind. If Tara wasn't who she said she was, then how could he trust anything she told him? More than deceived, he felt betrayed, and the only consolation was that his instincts had been correct.

He went back into the bedroom and immediately started to get dressed.

"Where're you going?" she said.

"Back to the cottage."

"Why?"

He continued without answering, and when he walked out, she got up, following him.

"What is it? What's wrong?"

"I gotta go."

"James, please—"

When she touched his arm, he spun around.

"Why did you come out here?"

"I told you," she said. "To watch my auntie's property—"

"Don't lie to me, goddammit!"

As he struggled with his coat, she grabbed him again, and he shoved her away.

"Let me go...Gwendolyn!"

Her face dropped and she stepped back.

"Don't call me that."

"Go to hell."

"Don't call me that," she said again, tears beginning to come down her cheeks.

"Isn't that your name?"

"That *was* my name."

James shook his head, spoke with a low disgust.

"I'm done with playing games."

As he went towards the door, Tara shot forward and got in his way.

"Fine!" she shouted. "You want the truth?"

"Doesn't everyone?"

"My husband was killed," she said, sobbing openly. "He was with the IRA, I had no idea. They were making a bomb, it went off prematurely. Another man died as well, three others were arrested..."

He hated to see her so hysterical, but he found the story strangely intriguing, and war was always something he could relate to.

"...I went home for the funeral. Kevin was from Belfast too, except he was a Catholic..."

He realized then that Tara—or Gwendolyn—was Protestant, a side of the conflict and a community that he didn't hear much about in the American press.

"...Some men contacted my sister's boyfriend," she went on. "They were from the Ulster Defense Force. They said I needed to go into hiding—"

"Why?" James interrupted.

"The IRA might think I would talk, that I would be a witness against the three survivors." Tara stopped to breathe, shaking her head so hard that tears went flying. "I don't know what they would want from me, I had no idea Kevin was—"

Suddenly, a knock. James froze. Tara put her hands to her mouth. After what she had just told him, it changed all the implications of an unexpected visitor in a storm. He wasn't scared, or even nervous, and fear was a luxury for people who still had a lot to lose. He worried about Tara, however, and would do anything to defend her.

He held his finger to his lips, motioned for her to step back. He scanned the room quickly and grabbed the poker from beside the fireplace. It wasn't easy to wield, but it could strike and stab, and a rudimentary weapon was better than no weapon at all.

He went back over to the door and, raising the cast-iron bar, he reached for the knob, ready for anything.

"Sir?"

Standing there were the three boys from across the hill, their faces red and rain sheeting down their plastic ponchos. James was relieved that it wasn't assassins, but he could still tell something was wrong.

"What is it?"

"Sir," the oldest said, out of breath. "Your dog...he...he got swept off the beach..."

Before they could say another word, James glanced behind to Tara then was gone. He ran down the road, blinded by the rain and stumbling over the rough ground. At one point, he tripped on something and landed flat in a puddle. But he got up and continued, past the cottage and towards the shore, and when he reached the top of the bluff, he stopped. Below, the sea and coastline fought for terrain like ancient enemies, waves surging over the land and the headlands fending them off. The beach was all but swallowed up, a thin strip of sand like the last gasp of a dying soldier.

James heard a noise, the unmistakable bark of Rod somewhere in all the chaos. He charged towards the water, kicking off his boots and diving in, momentarily stunned by the cold. A wave knocked him from the side and sent him into a tumble. When he righted himself, he gasped for air and called for Rod, who answered with a distant cry. James swam in that direction, punching through the swells, fighting against the storm with all the pent-up fury of his years of resentment and regret.

The undertow was, at moments, inescapable, and each time he went down, he wasn't sure he would come back up. Not long ago, he would have chosen to succumb, slipped willingly into the depths, leaving behind neither a body nor a memory. All that was changed now, however, and with Tara he no longer didn't care if he lived or died. In the howling confusion of the darkness and disorder, everything became suddenly clear.

When he reached the crest of a wave, he spotted something splashing and went towards it.

"Rod!" he screamed, choking on saltwater.

He swam with his head down because it was faster, looking up every few seconds, fixated on the spot where he last saw him. But each time he got to it, the dog was gone. Then there was another faint call from somewhere else, an illusion he couldn't seem to catch.

"I'm coming, boy!"

James was never sure Rod was real anyway, wondering at times whether he was Sergeant Rodriguez incarnate or some angel sent to damn or redeem him. But he loved the animal more than himself and so fought with all the desperate strength of a man trying to save his own child.

A giant wave crashed over him, spinning him around, and he struggled to get to the surface.

"Rod!"

This time there was no response.

A swell hit him from behind, another head on. Attacked from all sides, James fended them off until, finally, he could fend them off no more. He turned to head back to shore, his body limp and mind disoriented, but realized it was too far. Then—blackness.

Seventeen

JAMES SQUINTED IN THE WHITE LIGHT, HIS HEAD THROBBING and mouth parched. Even before he moved, he could tell he was hurt, a pain so generalized that he couldn't pinpoint any one location. When he tried to sit up, a soft hand touched his shoulder, urging him back to the bed. He thought it was Tara until his eyes adjusted and he saw the smiling face of a young nurse, her hair tucked under a white cap. Irish girls all looked the same, he thought, with dark hair and lips as red as roses.

"Keep still, Luv," she said.

He nodded and put his head back, the sound of machines clicking and beeping around him. There was an IV in his left arm—a blood pressure cuff around his right. He could tell he was under sedation, that woozy haze that felt like controlled hallucination. It was the same feeling he had the last time he woke up in a hospital over a decade before after his point man went to take a piss and stepped on a mosquito mine, killing him instantly. The explosion also injured a half dozen other men, including James, who caught a volley of searing hot shrapnel to the right side. He probably would have died too, the medic told him, but for some reason, he had chosen to wear his flak jacket that day. His life had always been like that, he thought, the smallest decisions, the most minute changes having the greatest effect.

As he lay still, his mind drifted to the present, and he began to think about why he was there. Much of what happened was still foggy, like the faint and scattered recollections of a drunken night. He recalled being at Tara's house, having sex on her couch then moving to the bedroom, arguing in the kitchen, a knock at the door, running through the rain, falling several times, the frigid ocean water, the darkness, the horror.

"Mr. Dunford?"

When he looked up, a doctor was standing over him, a man in his mid-fifties with a white beard and glasses. James nodded and tried to speak but his throat was too dry.

"Alva," he said to the nurse, "some water, please."

Alva. Hearing his ex-wife's name, James grinned but was otherwise unmoved. The coincidences in his life were too many not to think that some force or fate wasn't trying to get his attention.

The nurse came back with a small paper cup and held it to his lips, and he drank.

"What happened?" he said to the doctor, his voice hoarse.

"You decided to take a swim last weekend...in a hurricane."

"Last weekend?"

"You've been here nearly a week."

James sighed, as incredulous as he was disappointed.

"My dog. I...I was trying to save him—"

"And you did."

He looked sharply at the doctor and their eyes met.

"You're both damn lucky," the man said. "There was a fisherman in the area. He plucked you two out."

James swallowed, so emotional he had to look away. As he gazed out the window, the buildings of University Hospital in Galway looked like a small metropolis. The sun was bright, the sky clear, and for once it felt like a new day. He didn't know if what he felt was joy, relief, or gratitude —or some combination of the three—but it was the closest he had come to tears in a long time.

"Now," the doctor said. "We can account for the hypoxia, but what are these lesions?"

James glanced down at his arm and chuckled—of all the injuries he ever got, the bitemarks seemed to be taking the longest to heal.

"From a dog, a different dog...a wild dog."

"When was the last time you had a tetanus shot?"

"Probably boot camp."

The man winced, like he might have understood but wasn't sure.

"In the Marines," James explained. "'67."

The doctor turned to the young woman and said, "Order a booster."

She nodded with a smile and notated it on a clipboard.

"Doc, when can I go?"

"Hopefully in the morning, as long as your oxygen levels are fine. We've asked your girlfriend to bring some clothing."

"My girlfriend?"

The doctor glanced over at the nurse, who responded with an embarrassed hesitation.

"I assumed she was your sweetheart," she said. "She's been here every day."

* * *

Tara pulled into the cottage and parked beside the garden to avoid the twigs and branches that still covered much of the yard. The storm had ravaged the shore, tearing up entire sections of beach grass and flooding low-lying fields. According to RTÉ, no one was killed but further up the coast, some cows had been swept out to sea.

She didn't have power for two days and had to live by fire and candlelight while trying to finish all her perishable food before it went bad. But she really wasn't hungry and had been a wreck all week, although in a different way than before. Gone were the sudden fits of panic and sleepless nights, replaced by a less selfish anxiety. She hadn't known that feeling since Kevin was alive, and it was comforting to be able to worry about someone other than herself again.

As Tara walked up to the cottage, she felt sneaky going in without James. Whether it was all the repairs he had done, or just the fact that he had stayed there, she would always associate it with him. She had only been by once since the incident, and it was to secure the door, using a piece of rusted wire until she could get a locksmith to drive out. At the time, they still didn't know if James was going to live, and as rational as she thought she was, some superstitious impulse kept her from crossing over the threshold. But he did survive, and now she had to get his things so she could bring him home.

She stepped inside and it was dark, the air thick with the unventilated fumes of turf that had burned a week ago. The house was so old it didn't have wall switches, and she had to go over and turn on a lamp. When the light came on, the first thing she noticed was James' typewriter sitting on the parlor table with a single sheet of paper like some dramatic scene of a solitary writer. Over at the kitchen, plates were piled high in the sink, and a milk carton sat empty on the counter. There was a pillow on the couch, a pair of socks on the floor, but otherwise, the place was as tidy as the day he moved in.

She walked down the short hall and into the bedroom, reaching for the lamp on the nightstand. The bed hadn't been slept in, and in the corner, his luggage was set against the wall. The room had a dresser, but she knew he wasn't using it because when she went over and opened the suitcase, all his clothes were in it. Staring at his things, laid bare like a summation of who he was, Tara got suddenly sentimental. She knew James had a difficult past, that he had seen some awful things, but it didn't explain why he came to Connemara. Of the many questions she had about his life, one rose above them all: *Was he running from something or towards something?*

As she knelt to gather some clothes, she began to sob. She took a pair of faded denim jeans and a wool sweater that was torn at the shoulder. She searched under the pile and also found a t-shirt and white Haines underwear, the same kind Kevin used to wear. Tara had just started to smile when her hand hit something hard and she froze. She pushed aside some things and saw the glistening steel of a handgun.

She sat breathless, staring at the weapon, tears falling from her eyes. She picked up the clothes, shut the suitcase, and ran back out to the parlor. Her body trembled; her mind whirled with thoughts she didn't want to think. When, by some instinct, she was drawn to the typewriter, she read the last sentence of the letter James had been working on and it all made horrific sense.

I can no longer live...

~

Tara made the trip to Galway in under two hours, racing down the N59, swerving around trucks and automobiles like she was being chased. The trip still seemed to take forever, but it gave her time to think of what she would say. Her emotions wavered between sadness, disappointment, outrage, and grief. Mixed somewhere in there was disgust, aimed as much at herself as it was at James because she, too, had considered the unthinkable. But thoughts were different than urges and urges different than actions. Despite her parents' piety, Tara never took to formalized religion, but she had been raised with enough Christian theology to know that suicide was the ultimate selfish act, the exact opposite of what Christ had intended.

When she barreled through the front doors of the hospital, orderlies, patients, and other personnel turned to look. She went over to the elevator bank, the bag of clothing in her arms, and got on. The doors opened on the third floor and she stepped out, quickly collecting herself so the nursing staff wouldn't be alarmed. She walked down the hallway and turned into the last room, where she saw James sitting up in the bed, reading a newspaper.

Still calm, she quietly closed the door, and he looked up.

"You cowardly bastard!"

His mouth fell open, the paper dropped to his lap.

"Tara?"

She went towards him, shaking her finger.

"That's why you moved out here?"

"I have no idea what you're—"

"Leave everything behind, come back to the place you loved as a child, only to end it all? Full circle, huh? Like some fuckin' Hollywood movie?!"

When she paused to catch her breath, he got out of the bed, keeping his eyes on her in a way that, even in all the commotion, made her feel desired.

"I know," she continued, her anger softening to sadness, "what it's like to hurt, James, what it's like to not see any future, what it's like to..."

She stopped because she couldn't go on and sank into quiet convulsions of sobbing, staring at the floor, despondent and afraid. Unlike her sister, she had always been sensible, going off to college and trying to start a new life in London. Yet the madness seemed to follow her, and she couldn't help but think she was cursed.

Tara didn't look, but she could hear James approaching, felt his warmth as he got near. In one sudden swoop, he took her in his arms and hugged her, and she cried into his shoulder.

"It's not what you think," he said.

"I found the gun."

"I take it everywhere. Always have since the war."

"But the letter—"

"Letter?"

"In the typewriter. It said *I can no longer live*."

He pulled her tighter, rubbed her back.

"It wasn't finished," he said, almost in a whisper. "...I can no longer live *hiding from my past*. It's to the mother of a guy in my platoon, to explain how he died. It's bothered me for years."

She stared up, her vision blurry, and saw that he was clean-shaven for the first time. The sight of his bare skin, a mosaic of blemishes, scars, marks, and wrinkles, seemed to capture all the parts of his troubled life. And the fact that there was still some smoothness meant there was still a future. Tara knew then that, not only did she love him, but that he loved her too.

"Tell me you wouldn't do it."

James didn't hesitate, but she shook him for an answer anyway.

"Never."

Eighteen

THE WIND WHIPPED ACROSS THE ROAD AS THEY CAME
through the mountains, so strong that, at moments, James could feel
the car being pulled to one side or the other. Outside was bitter cold, the
sky a misty gray, the sort of weather that would have meant snow back
in Boston. It had been a long time since he was in a car with a woman
behind the wheel, and his ex-wife never even had a license. Nevertheless,
he trusted Tara, and she drove so carefully it was adorable, both hands
on the wheel and eyes fixed on the road. She was quiet too, and James
appreciated the silence because he was still recovering.

He didn't know how much seawater he ingested, but he had a
constant headache and got dizzy if he moved around too much or too
quickly. Somewhere in his midsection was a mild pain, and he always
feared some shrapnel from the war could get knocked loose and go
floating around his body, ravaging him a second time. Either way, the
storm that night took more out of him than any march or firefight, and
although his attempt to save Rod might have been brave, it was also
foolish because he never was a good swimmer.

When they turned off the main road, he was glad to finally be back,
and being away made him realize that the small cottage on the peninsula
was the closest thing he had to a home.

"James?" Tara said.

He looked ahead and saw several vehicles parked by the entrance to the property.

"Who's this?"

"That's Paddy Coyne's truck," she said. "He saved you."

They squeezed between the cars, which were tight up against the hedgerows, and when they turned into the yard, they were met by a crowd of smiling faces. The only person James recognized was the fisherman, and he wondered if they all knew when he was due to arrive or if it had been a lucky guess. Considering the insignificance of time out here, he thought, it probably didn't matter.

James got out and walked towards Paddy, who stood with his arms crossed and chewing the tip of his pipe. He tried to think of something cute or clever, but when he approached, his sincerity overcame any attempt to lighten the gravity of what he had to say. He held out his hand and looked the man directly in the eye.

"Thank you."

"You're mighty welcome," Paddy said. "It was a bit of redemption for me personally. I lost me two uncles to a gale in '27."

"The sea can be merciless."

"As can humankind."

James paused, struck by the wisdom of the statement.

"What were you doing out there?" he asked.

"Me boat had come untethered. I was trying to get it to port in Cleggan."

"And did you?"

"Indeed," Paddy said, looking at the others. "And with a bigger catch than expected."

Everyone laughed, and James forced a grin, his cheeks twitching with fatigue and emotion. Standing in the group was a younger man with a camera around his neck, and James didn't notice him until he stepped forward.

"Mr. Dunford," he said. "I'm with the Connemara Tribune. Would you pose for a photo?"

James consented with a reluctant nod because, as much as he didn't want the attention, he couldn't say no. Paddy came beside him and they stood together, hands clasped and holding their smiles. The moment the shutter snapped, James heard a bark, and when he turned around, Paddy's nephews walked into the yard. And there behind them, his snout down and scampering through the weeds, was Rod. Once he noticed his master, he let out a great cry and darted forward, rearing in the air and circling James uncontrollably.

"Hey, boy. Settle down."

He knelt down, and Rod began to lick his face, the most poignant reception he had ever received. He ran his hands through the dog's mane, feeling the lumps and imperfections of his old, ragged body. Rod's nose was still scabbed from the fight, but his eyes were clear, and he looked healthy.

When James got back up, Tara was getting his clothes out of the car, the denim jeans, leather belt, flannel shirt, and socks he had on when he was pulled from the water. Stiff with salt crystals, they needed to be washed twice, and he would have thrown them out had she not insisted on taking them. With Rod alive, he didn't want to be reminded of that night, the risks of attempting a rescue in darkness during a storm, and he evaluated it like a military mission. Nonetheless, Rod was alive and, more importantly, Tara didn't have to suffer through the rest of winter alone on this barren peninsula. It was a sentiment that James, despite his fondness for her, didn't quite expect.

"If you gentlemen don't mind," he said, "it's been a helluva week."

"Not at all," Paddy said.

Tara came over and together they walked towards the cottage.

"Sir," the reporter said. "Are you the same James Dunford who received the Medal of Honor in 1971?"

James glanced at Tara then slowly turned around. In those few seconds, it seemed like the entire community—the entire world—was waiting for his reply. He could have lied, but he was tired of trying to change the past by ignoring it, and sometimes denying your valor was just as pretentious as wearing it on your sleeve.

"Yeah," he said. "That was me."

The boys looked at each other and their faces beamed. James hated a lot of things about himself, and for years he felt the value of the commendation never made up for the cost of Sergeant Rodriquez's life.

But if the medal could inspire a few young kids, he thought, maybe it was all worth it.

James untied the wire that was holding the door closed, telling himself he would fix it in the morning. When he walked in, the first thing he did, even before he turned on a light, was put some turf in the fireplace and light it. After a week in the sterile confines of the hospital, he yearned for the sweet smell of Irish earth, the putrefaction of millennia, the burning bones of his ancestors.

As he moved the briquettes around with the poker, Rod came over and lay down. James turned back to Tara, who stood quietly by the door holding the bag.

"Please, make yourself at home," he said.

"Where should I put these?"

"In the bedroom, if you don't mind."

When she stepped away, he reached over to the table where, beside the typewriter, sat a sealed white envelope. It was the most significant letter he had written, and it didn't require an address. He snatched it up and threw it on the fire, watching as it curled into ash, mesmerized by the flames.

As a boy, he had stood in this very spot with his brother and cousins, dressed in pajamas and roasting marshmallows while they all discussed, with perfect seriousness, some recent experience or discovery, a spiral seashell, beehive, or newborn calf, the infinite mysteries of nature. Those were the best days, or so he always imagined, that immutable perfection of childhood innocence.

"Is something wrong?" Tara asked.

James turned and she was standing at the corner.

"Nothing."

"Would you like me to make some tea?"

"Tea," he said, with a tense, emotional smile. "That sounds good."

Nineteen

～

IT WAS A BEAUTIFUL WINTER DAY, SOMETHING THAT AFTER
the weeks of gray gloom, seemed hard to imagine. The sky was a sheet of
faded blue, interrupted only by a few clouds above the distant mountains. For Tara, it would have been pleasant if she wasn't so anxious and
for the whole ride, she stared ahead with breathless impatience. She
could have taken a pill, but her agitation was from excitement and not
sadness, and either way, she no longer wanted the empty relief of booze
and prescription drugs.

She turned onto the gravel road and continued past her house,
pulling into the cottage so fast the car bounced and almost gave her
whiplash. In the field beyond, she saw a group of young boys leaning on
the fence, idling in their school uniforms. They had been coming in
droves, many of them locals but some from as far away as Clifden and
Roundstone. News that an American war hero was living here had
spread, making James a minor celebrity.

As Tara got out, the front door opened and James came out, Rod
scurrying behind him. The stubble on his chin was clearer in the sun,
and she wondered if he was going to let it grow out again. They
approached each other, and she noticed in his expression the same

subtle grin that she had, the giddy knowledge of all they had done and shared. Since he got out of the hospital, they had slept together every night, and although no longer awkward, their daily interactions contained all the sly glances and secret innuendo of a new romance.

"I stopped by earlier."

"I was in Galway," Tara said, and before he could ask why, she added, "I brought you this."

She held out a copy of the Connacht Tribune, where across the front page was a bold headline:

LOCAL HERO SAVES AMERICAN HERO

Beside it was a picture of James and Paddy shaking hands, Tara diagonally behind them and at an angle she didn't find flattering. She never expected to be in it, and she always hated having her photo taken.

"It's from last week," she said.

"Explains a lot."

He raised his eyebrows and glanced over at the boys with a sarcastic smirk. He was trying to be considerate, but he didn't like the attention, and Tara knew that, in the complex list of reasons why he had come to Connemara, privacy was near the top.

"Let's go for a walk," she said.

"Sure."

They went out of the yard and headed towards the main road, crossing over and continuing up the path, past scattered cottages, cow fields, a tiny stream. Soon they started to ascend and, with the ground dry after a week of sun and no rain, it was easier to walk on. When Tara first moved here, she hiked the mountain almost every day, and the open space seemed the only antidote to her grief. Kevin's death had knocked the wind out of her and not just metaphorically because at times she felt like she was suffocating.

Halfway up, James stopped and turned, hands on his hips and staring out. Facing north, the coastline was clear for miles, an endless expanse of hills and valleys. Even at this altitude, there was hardly any wind, and the sea was flat from the shore to Inishturk, deceivingly harmless in its stillness. Tara could tell he was panting by the steam from his breath, but knowing he was probably too stubborn to rest, she spared him his pride and said, "Can we sit for a couple of minutes?"

They stepped over to a rocky outcropping, and Rod took off across the hillside. She had wanted to wait until they were at the top, as if greater heights brought greater significance. But when they sat down, she saw no point, and the nervous anticipation she had carried with her since Galway was wearing her down.

Tara looked at James, who sat quietly, fidgeting with his hands. They had been more intimate in the last week than most couples were in a year, and yet in tender moments, he wilted like a self-conscious adolescent. Despite his tough exterior, he was sensitive at heart, something she felt the first time they met. She knew also he wasn't one for subtlety or frills which was why, when it came to what she had to say, she saw no reason to be anything but blunt.

"James, I'm pregnant."

He blinked once, tilted his head.

"That so?"

When she nodded, his face broke out into a full and heartfelt smile. She had promised herself she wouldn't cry, but the moment she saw his reaction, she couldn't avoid it.

"That's about the best news I've had...ever."

She laughed so loud that Rod looked up from the grass.

"Are you happy?" she said.

"More than you know."

Tara shook her head, sniffling and jittery with emotion. Although she wanted to hear more, it was enough for now, and it was getting late. Shadows were forming between the rocks and vales—the day was coming to an end. Over the next ridge, she could see the orange and yellow glow of the sinking sun. She wiped her eyes and jumped up with a playful grin.

"Let's go!" she said.

"Where to?"

"The top. Hurry!"

She took off up the hill, waving for him to follow.

"Can't you wait up?" he said.

"I can. But the sunset won't..."

Twenty

JAMES STOOD OUTSIDE IN THE DARKNESS, A CIGARETTE IN HIS
mouth. The sky was clear, stars gleaming over the black ocean, and it
was so cold that even Rod opted to stay in by the fire. Tara had told him
that he could smoke in the house, and she even went so far as to get him
some clamshells to use as ashtrays. But knowing that she hated the smell,
he wouldn't make her suffer the consequences of his own bad habits.
They had enough things to adjust to, he thought, learning to accommo-
date each other's quirks and routines, and living together was a whole
lot different than staying over a few days a week. She went to bed around
10 p.m. and then was up all night; he stayed up much later, but once he
was asleep nothing could wake him. She was a light eater all around, but
while he could forego breakfast with a little coffee and nicotine, he abso-
lutely had to have lunch. Whenever they went out for a walk, she
preferred to hike, and all he wanted to do was stroll along the beach.

James was technically still renting the cottage, if only because he had
already paid Tara's aunt in advance. And with the exception of his
toothbrush, coat, and wallet, he kept all his stuff there, and it was more
about space than some cynical fallback plan. The arrangement reminded
him of his ex-wife, those heady days of early courtship when they each
had their own apartment, he with his brother in a rental property their

father owned and she with some roommates from her one and only semester at Boston State College. When, less than a year later, they merged their homes and thus their lives, James learned that love moved fast.

His marriage didn't so much dissolve as fade away. Long after his brother made it clear he wouldn't share ownership of the business, James continued to work at *Dunford & Sons Construction*, mostly as a project foreman. He always told himself he stayed on out of stubbornness, but the truth was he thought he had nowhere else to go, the war having stolen from him his best years. A bitterness had been planted inside him that grew each year, and by the time he became aware of it, it had taken over his soul like an invasive weed. If he wasn't irritable, he was withdrawn. When he and his wife spent a week in Hampton Beach one summer, he stayed in the cottage the whole time, drinking cheap beer and watching the Watergate hearings. She tried—God knows she tried—even suggesting they go to see a marriage counselor. But he would have none of that new-age crap, which he saw as more Hippie decadence, and so he was content in his misery, feeling that the world had done him wrong. When his wife finally walked out on him, he was actually happy for her.

James flicked his cigarette, and as he turned to go back in, he saw headlights at the top of the road. With the house and the cottage the only two residences, no one came down there at night so he walked over to see who it was. Moments later, a truck rolled up and it was Paddy Coyne.

"Mr. Dunford," he said, quickly getting out. "Are ye alone?"

"What's wrong?"

"Some men," he said, his voice low, jittery. "At Joyce's. They were asking after Tara."

"What men?"

"I don't know. They're not from these parts anyway."

He stared at Paddy, whose fleshy eyes shone nervously in the moonlight.

"Joyce's you say?"

"Three of them."

James thanked him and walked back to the house, opening the door quietly, Rod looking over from the fireplace. He grabbed his wool coat off the hook and was just about to leave when he heard, "Who was that?"

He turned around and Tara was standing in her robe in the shadow of the hallway, her hair tousled and eyes sleepy.

"Paddy Coyne."

"What's he doing here at this hour?"

He hesitated, and although he didn't want to lie, he also didn't want to panic her.

"He said there's a light on in the cottage. I'm going to turn it off."

James drove down the long and desolate road, the coastline dark except for a few scattered homes. His mind wandered as he went, staring over at the magnificent night sky, his thoughts ranging from *how far away is the moon?* to *I wonder if fish sleep at night.* He had been like that since the war and maybe before, distracted when he needed to be the most alert. It wasn't that he didn't get afraid, but that he was able to separate himself from the fear, feeling it without being crippled by it. Whether it was a skill or some defect of his biology, he could never tell, and all he knew was that it had been useful in combat but bad for love.

James slowed as he came around the bend into the village. The only lights were at Joyce's and the small hostel at the corner. He pulled into the alleyway between the shops and parked in the shadows. He reached under the passenger seat for his .38 revolver, checking the chamber then tucking it in the side of his waist. He got out and walked towards the street, his collar up and hands in his pockets, and as he approached Joyce's, he glanced in the window to see Jerry behind the bar, three men seated in front of him. One had on a plaid jacket, the other two, leather coats, and their sateen shirts were a far cry from the drab cotton and flannel of local fashion. Such styles might have been common in summer, but tourist season was months away, and it was obvious that they weren't from around there.

James stopped at the door, breathing deep and organizing his thoughts before entering. It was a ritual similar to the one he and his men practiced in Vietnam, a short meditation before going on patrol or into battle.

When he stepped inside, everyone turned. He walked over to the bar, where Jerry stood cleaning a glass, his expression strained like he was trying to hide some worry or discomfort. Behind him, the television was on but muted, and the late news showed images of the political turmoil in the North. With Bobby Sands a week into his hunger strike, there were street protests in Dublin and Belfast, people holding placards in support of IRA prisoners.

"We're closing soon," Jerry said.

"I won't be long."

"What'll it be?"

"Ginger ale."

Jerry raised his eyebrows and the men briefly stopped talking. When one of them cracked a joke, James glanced over for the first time. They were all in their early twenties, with long hair and mustaches, the kind of look that was popular in the States a decade before. He didn't know if they were thugs, but he could tell they were street-hardened by their wiry frames, the way they spoke. He would soon find out, however, and if there was any way to gain the advantage in conversation, it was by speaking first.

"Here on holidays?" James said.

The man closest to him looked over with a smirk.

"Maybe. You from America?"

James shrugged his shoulders.

"Maybe."

"That Ronald Regan is a feckin' tyrant."

James smiled and took a sip of his soda.

"He was good in Knute Rockne," he said.

They all chuckled, although James wasn't convinced that they got the reference.

"What brings you out here, mate?"

"I met a woman."

"Those farm girls have a way, don't they?"

"Actually, she's from Belfast."

The other two guys went silent—a sudden tension filled the room.

Jerry looked over from the register, where he had been counting money, then conveniently found a reason to go out back. The man beside James took a long drag on his cigarette, staring through the smoke as it left his mouth.

"Oh yeah?" he said coldly. "And what's her name?"

"You wouldn't know her."

"You might be surprised."

"She's a quiet girl."

The man glanced back to his cohorts, who were now watching, listening.

"Introduce us," he said. "Let us be the judge of that."

James snickered to himself, taking another sip and wondering why the Ginger Ale there was so much more bitter than back home. The conversation was curt, but it wasn't clever, and the man had revealed too much already. James didn't know much about the IRA, its structure or its methods, but this was hardly the finesse of agents or special ops.

"Maybe we'll introduce ourselves..."

James stiffened, a chill went up his back. Leaning against the bar, he slowly turned and stared at them all at once. The first two men were unimpressed—or so they seemed—but the last one looked unsure and that was good, he thought, because he knew what he was up against.

"That wouldn't be a smart idea," he said.

"Your opinion doesn't fuckin' matter here."

As James stood facing them, he felt the onset of a manic anger that he had hoped to avoid. But when he looked into the first man's eyes, he saw a coldness that, up until a few weeks before, he himself had. He knew nothing about these young men, their suffering or their losses, and everyone caught up in a war experiences suffering and loss. The fact that he felt some distant sympathy for them meant that, after all these years, he was finally healing, he was becoming human again. In those few, short, tense seconds, he found himself getting emotional, and he even had the strange urge to thank them. But instead, he reached into the side of his jacket.

"He's got a!—"

Before the man could announce it, James whipped out the .38, grabbed him by the collar, and put the gun to his forehead.

"Drop your fucking weapons or I'll smoke him!"

When the other two hesitated, he pulled the trigger back until it clicked. Somberly, they reached in their coats and held up their pistols.

"Drop 'em!" James shouted. "Kick them across the floor."

No sooner had they complied than Jerry walked out from the back and, seeing what was happening, he immediately threw up his hands. James frowned, waved for him to lower them.

"You don't know what you're doin'," the first man said, the barrel pressed into the wrinkles of his skin.

"Get your C.O. on the phone," James said.

"What?"

"Get your C.O. on the phone."

"I can't—"

"Now!"

One of the other men looked at Jerry, who nodded, and then he came around the bar, James watching him carefully. Jerry handed him the phone, the man dialed a number, and everyone waited. James' adrenaline raged—his senses were so heightened he heard things that weren't there. But he wasn't hallucinating or losing his nerve, and he had total control over the situation. If anyone made a move, he knew exactly how he would kill them and in which order.

Finally, someone picked up and there was a short, whispered conversation. The man held out the phone to James, who took it and told him to stay behind the counter.

"Hello?"

"You got a lotta bollocks holdin' up my men," James heard in a deep, nasal Northern accent.

"Leave Tara alone. She knows nothing."

"You listen to me," he snapped. "I don't take orders from you! You don't even know her real name."

"Gwendolyn Evers."

"Then you know what happened to her husband."

"I know enough."

With each exchange, the man's words grew sharper, his voice more intense.

"We need to talk to her about that...situation."

"I'm afraid I can't let that happen."

Finally, the commander lost his patience.

"Do you wanna fuckin' die, mate?!"

"I'll take these bastards with me," James said.

"You do and you won't get five kilometers."

"Don't bother. I'll wait here for you."

"Who the hell is this?"

"Lieutenant James Dunford, 3rd U.S. Marines."

The man stopped, almost like he was stumped, and James was proud to know his service counted for something, even in a foreign country. Seconds passed, maybe a minute, before the commander spoke again, and when he did, he was calmer, almost conciliatory.

"I know who you are," he said with a sigh. "Is...is she your girlfriend?"

"You might say that."

The man paused.

"You've put me in an awkward position."

"Likewise," James said.

"We can't have snitches—"

"You won't."

Another pause.

"You have to understand, mate. We're at war."

Behind the man's bravado, James could sense a private torment, the need to explain or justify the violence he committed or experienced. He knew that angst and maybe, he thought, that was why the commander confided in him.

"Put Padraig back on, please," he said, and James assumed he meant the one who had dialed.

They talked for a minute before the guy handed the phone back.

"Lower your gun," the man said. "Tony's gonna back away slowly. Let the other two get their weapons. Don't make any sudden moves."

James followed his instructions as he spoke, and it was easier to defuse a situation when one person was directing. After gathering their things, the men walked out with no grumbling or threatening stares, and James was impressed by how well trained they were.

"They're gone."

"Good," the commander said. "Now, do us all a favor and make sure Ms. Evers stays out of Belfast."

"I can do that."

"And Lieutenant?" he said, and James listened closely. "God be with you."

With that, the man hung up, leaving him to wonder about the strange parting words. James never thought much about hidden meanings but considering how fortunate he had been in recent weeks, the comment was as much an observation of fact as it was a salutation.

He handed the phone across to Jerry, who stood looming in the shadow at the end of the bar. Jerry seemed relieved but only mildly, as if his concern all along was for his business and not his life. People out here trusted the IRA, they didn't fear it. James always knew the risks of confronting the men, and if things had gone differently—if he had been hurt or killed—the authorities would have been hard struck to find a witness.

"Would you like your mail before you go?"

James laughed quietly at the question, and it was a fitting anticlimax.

"Sure."

Jerry walked over and searched through the cubbies, coming back with a single envelope. In the dim light, James looked at the return address and nearly gasped when he saw the name: Elma Rodriguez. It was a letter he never expected to see, and the fact that she had written back meant as much as anything she could possibly say. He would read it in the morning with his coffee because he had no more courage left tonight.

James thanked Jerry and left so he could close up. Outside the air was crisp, and there was an almost perfect silence. He looked around the small village, the quiet homes and shops, the dark hills in the distance, and felt in no great rush to get back. As a boy, his mother called Connemara the *ends of the earth*, to which his father would reply *and the beginning of heaven*. Maybe it was true, James thought, and what better place to start a new life.

End

Purchase the rest of Jonathan Cullen's Shadows of Our Time collection, or turn the page for a sneak peak!

Storm Beyond the Tides:

https://www.amazon.com/dp/B09BM419DK

Bermuda Blue:

https://www.amazon.com/dp/B09L5DW67C

The Storm Beyond the Tides

CHAPTER 1

ELLIE AMES STOOD AT THE EDGE OF THE DOCK, A CRATE OF tools beside her, while her father worked on the motor, his forearms red and streaked with grease. Jack cared for the twenty-foot sloop like it was his, but he was only captaining it for a commercial outfit in Portland, getting paid a percentage of the catch, beholden to an owner he never met. He once had his own boat, before Mary got sick, and Ellie knew that working for someone else hurt his pride, tore at his soul, made every day a living penance for his past mistakes.

"Wrench," he said.

She got one from the box and handed it to him. Standing at the helm behind her, dressed in a smock and cap, was Benjamin Frazier, a family friend who had been working with Jack for several seasons.

"Hammer."

Ellie gave him one and Jack reached back without looking. As he crouched, his shirt lifted and she saw the scars on his back, as hideous in appearance as they were for the injury they represented. She still cringed at the sight of it, as did Mary, although the disfigurement had always been there and was as much a part of him as his dark beard and slight limp.

Finally, Jack sat up and sighed. Squinting in the morning sun, he held out the broken rubber belt like it was evidence from a crime scene, then looked at Ellie.

"Go to Lavery's," he said. "Get a new one."

She nodded and waved to Mary, who was leaning over the dock on her crutches, searching for minnows and jellyfish. They walked up the gangway, and when they came to the pier, Monk Island was bustling for the Fourth of July. Throngs of people—locals, vacationers, and day-trippers—filled the small waterfront and village, browsing the shops and lingering on the sidewalks. American flags hung from every lamppost and in every shop window. On the grassy slope overlooking the docks, people were already claiming spots for the evening fireworks over Portland Harbor. Young boys hawked souvenir brass lobster trinkets, and an old man dressed like Uncle Sam was selling maps for a nickel. There were vendor carts with roasted peanuts, cotton candy, and frankfurters, and the small port had the festive air of an outdoor carnival.

Ellie and Mary passed the terminal, where a ferry had just arrived and passengers were streaming off with suitcases and bags, beach chairs and umbrellas. As they merged with the crowd and headed up towards the village, something caught Ellie's attention and she got distracted. It was a boy, or young man—much like herself, he was in that period of life that skirted the line between youth and adulthood. He was tall and thin, with short-cropped hair and a linen shirt, and he walked alongside his parents, pulling two suitcases. His father limped with a cane, a cigar in hand and scarf around his neck—unusual attire for summer—and his mother was a petite brunette with a flowered dress and pearls around her neck. Monk Island drew visitors from everywhere, but there was something mysterious about the family, and Ellie couldn't stop staring.

"What're you looking at?"

Ellie turned to Mary, who looked up with a toothy grin.

"Um, nothing. Thought I recognized someone."

The "village" on Monk Island was little more than a small intersection with a grocer, butchery, ice cream parlor, and some tourist shops which sold souvenirs, hats, and postcards. But as the only commercial area, people spoke of it like it was a metropolis. On one corner was The Devonshire, an inn and wedding hall that had once been the summer estate of a nineteenth-century oil baron. Behind it, on the dirt road leading up the hill, was the American Legion, opened after the First World War when the Portland post became full. Farther down Gull Avenue was the Bowladrome, a twelve-lane bowling alley that was once a fish salting facility. With its big neon sign, it was the closest thing to glamor on the island, and young people, both locals and tourists, flocked there on summer nights.

Lavery's Delicatessen was a combination hardware store and bait & tackle shop that catered to the island's fishermen. On an island with such sparse commerce, every business had to maximize what it offered. Once an actual delicatessen, Lavery's was owned by their neighbor, Joe Mallet Jr., who bought it cheap during the Depression and never changed the sign.

When Ellie opened the door, a bell overhead jingled. Inside, the shop was dry and dusty, with wide-plank floors whose nails were worn shiny from boots. The walls had bins filled with galvanized fasteners, and a chain scale hung from the ceiling. The shelves were stocked with gallons of deck paint, spar-varnish, pine buoys, coils of line. In one corner was a stack of slat & leather-hinged lobster pots, in the other, the more modern wire traps. There were wooden oars of all sizes, cotton cordage, toggle buoys, and gaff hooks. Combined with all the bait in the storeroom, Lavery's had everything a fisherman would want, and Jack once remarked that there was enough gear to outfit the Phoenicians.

Ellie walked towards the counter while Mary wandered over to look at things. The smell of pine-tar oakum caulk, turpentine, and kerosene was awful, and Ellie had to hold her breath. She tried not to wince, but when Kate looked up from behind the register, it was obvious she could tell.

"Ellie, you alright?"

"It's hot as toast out there," she said. "I need one of these."

Kate took the part and examined it. Although motorized sloops arrived in the early '30s, mechanization was still a fascination on an island where half the boats used sails.

"Daddy!" she called out.

Kate was the only girl Ellie knew who still called her father *Daddy*. They had been friends since either of them could remember, and Kate lived just down the hill from her in a cottage by Drake's Cove. Jack grew up with her father and uncles, and the Ames and Mallet families had been close for generations. Kate was pretty in a plain way, with sandy-colored hair and blue eyes that she inherited from an Irish great-grandfather.

Moments later, Joe Mallet came out from the storeroom, his shirt-sleeves rolled up, glasses tilted, sweating.

"Afternoon, Ellie," he said.

"Good afternoon, Mr. Mallet."

He approached the counter, wiping his hands with a rag, and when his daughter held up the belt, he squinted.

"Lemme check."

While he went out back to look, Ellie and Kate waited, and for the first time in their lives, they had nothing to talk about. With Kate's acceptance to nursing school in Lewiston, something had changed between them, and Ellie didn't know if what she felt was sadness or envy. They had just graduated in May from Portland High, where for four years they took the ferry together every day. Some of the local boys in their class returned to work in fishing, but with the lobster industry still in a slump, many young people left Monk Island, finding jobs in the factories in Portland or moving out of Maine altogether.

"So? When do you leave?"

Before Kate could answer, something rattled and they both looked over.

"Mary!" Ellie snapped. "Leave that be!"

Leaning on her crutches, her sister stood beside a sloop motor, up on blocks and waiting to be repaired. Like everything related to fishing, it was rusted and covered in barnacles.

"It's no bother, Ellie. Let her look."

Ellie consented, but only because Kate didn't mind and, a moment later, Joe Mallet came out shaking his head.

"I'll have to order it. I could maybe have it before the weekend."

He seemed as disappointed at not having the part in stock as Jack would be when he found out, and Ellie dreaded having to tell him. Her father wouldn't blame her directly, but he would grumble, hiss, curse—throw a quiet tantrum that would make her feel somehow partly responsible.

"I'll let Father know. Thank you."

Joe Mallet returned to the backroom and Ellie called for Mary, who pried herself away from the motor, positioned her crutches, and headed for the door.

"Ellie," Kate said. "I'm off Saturday if you wanna go to the beach?"

When she hesitated, it wasn't because she couldn't decide, but that she might have to work on the boat.

"I'll have to see."

"Okay," Kate said. "Let me know."

Ellie held the door for Mary and they walked out. Going from the dim shop to outside was a shock to the eyes and, for a few seconds, she was blinded.

"Pardon?"

She heard a voice and, as the sunspots cleared, saw the young man from the ferry standing with his parents in the street. She acknowledged him with a courteous smile, and he walked over with his hands in his pockets.

"Would you happen to know where Thrush Lane is?"

The first thing she noticed was an accent, and she wasn't surprised because Monk Island got visitors from everywhere. The second was that he was taller than her father by at least three inches. His eyes were crystal-blue, his face smooth in a way that was handsome but not unmasculine. In a place where every male seemed to have a pug-nose and a scowl, he was almost debonair, and she felt self-conscious in her dirty dress and work shoes.

"Oh, yes, Thrush Lane," she said, stumbling. "Go up that road there, past the American Legion, to the top of the hill, then turn left."

As he repeated the directions, the young man looked at her and she felt herself start to blush.

"Thank you," he said, with a slight bow.

"My pleasure."

He backed away like he was retreating from a stage, his expression gracious yet somehow strained, and returned to his parents, who stood weary in the heat, their clothes wrinkled, shoulders slumped.

"He talks funny."

Ellie turned abruptly to Mary like she forgot she was beside her.

"They're from another country."

"What country?"

Ellie mumbled something, but it wasn't an answer because she didn't know. Instead, she watched as the family picked up their suitcases and began to walk. Just as they turned the corner onto Gull Avenue, the young man looked over and Ellie responded with a faint smile, but by then he was out of sight.

The cottage on Thrush Lane was a small clapboard house with a front porch and gabled windows. It was set back off the street, nestled among a scattering of birch trees and spruce. An old stone wall ran along one side, a colonial remnant from the days when Monk Island was farmland and pastures.

By the time the Brinks arrived, it was noon and the interior was stifling. Karl brought the luggage in, and they wandered through the rooms, separately and with a silent fascination, as if exploring an ancient tomb. Like any summer cottage, it was dank and drafty and smelled of must. The furniture was clean but shabby, a mismatch of wooden chairs, a wicker couch, a handmade coffee table, and floral curtains which appeared to be made from bedsheets or a tablecloth. On the walls were some old oil paintings—a seascape and a picture of a man on a bicycle—and coral shells were stacked above the windows.

As Karl peered in the pantry, he heard his mother in the next room say, "So simple."

He went out the back door to a small porch with three Adirondack chairs, a pedestal ashtray, and an empty beehive birdcage. The yard was overgrown with crabgrass and dandelions, and in the distance, he could see the next cottage through the trees. Standing at the threshold, he breathed in the salt air, smelled the wildflowers, listened to the low and constant hum of bees and other insects. The sensations of nature brought back fond memories of when he was just a boy and they vacationed at the seaside town of Lübeck.

"Karl!"

He ran back inside and up the stairs, and when he got to his parents' bedroom, his father was stooped over the luggage, panting and frustrated.

"Father?"

"Help me with this."

Karl lifted the suitcase and put it on the bed. As he went to undo the straps, Mr. Brink held out his hand.

"That's enough."

Karl flinched and stepped back, offended by the outburst but in no mood to argue. He stormed out of the room, down the narrow staircase, and into the kitchen, where his mother was going through the cabinet. She turned to him slowly, almost like she was in a trance, and held up a coffee can.

"The previous tenants left this. Can you believe it?"

"I'm sure they intended to."

She smelled inside, shook her head.

"At least half a pound."

Like anyone who had lived through the scarcity of the Weimar years, she hated wastefulness, but Karl knew that wasn't the only reason she was in a stupor.

"Come," he said, putting his arm around her. "You rest. I'll put these away."

"But I must organize things."

She tried to resist, but he urged her into the parlor and onto the couch, where he told her to lie down and then put a pillow under her head. Her hairline was damp, her cheeks flushed, and she was lethargic from the heat. Although they had opened some windows, Mr. Brink insisted the curtains remain closed, and Karl could tell it was trapping the warm air.

He grabbed her pocketbook from the table and, as he reached for a napkin, his hand brushed her pills. They had been prescribed in Germany by a doctor who told her to take one whenever she was "feeling gloomy." But the drugs had become more than an occasional comfort—she couldn't go a day without them—and Karl feared they were the cause of her problems and not the cure.

"What is this?"

He let go of the vial, shut the pocketbook, and turned to see his father in the doorway, dressed in his shirtsleeves, suspenders loose over his shoulders. Without a suit, Mr. Brink looked like a skeleton under a sheet, and Karl was surprised by how much weight he had lost.

"Mother is tired. She needs rest."

Mr. Brink nodded, then reached in his pocket and took out his wallet. As he opened it, Karl saw a thin stack of bills, mostly small denominations, their weekly allotment, the rest being in a bank in Portland. With restrictions on currency leaving Germany, they brought as much as they could, but it wasn't enough.

"Go to the butcher. Get some ham, cured if possible—"

"And beef," Mrs. Brink said, her voice shaky. "I can make a stew."

He gazed at his wife with a tender smile then handed Karl a five.

"Get as much as possible. Bargain, if you can."

Karl scoffed to himself, knowing that prices in America were fixed and not open to negotiation like some Arab bazaar. His father was a sophisticated man, he thought, but as the son of a cobbler from Munich, the naivety of his rural upbringing often showed.

"I will try."

"You must do more than try."

"Would someone please get me some water?" Mrs. Brink said, and they both looked over.

As Karl went to go into the kitchen, his father sidestepped and blocked his way.

"I'll get water—you get the food. And don't talk to anyone."

Their eyes locked in a quiet standoff that was cordial but no less tense. For Karl, every conversation with his father seemed confrontational, every interaction a competition of wills. He conceded for his mother's sake only and turned to leave when suddenly—boom!

They all jumped, and Mr. Brink stood stunned, his eyes darting and arms out, prepared for something much worse than what it was.

"What in God's name was that?!" he said.

For a man who was a committed atheist, he blasphemed more than anyone Karl knew.

"Fireworks, Father. It's American Independence Day."

Mr. Brink swallowed and nodded, looking away as if embarrassed, and Karl went towards the door.

"Son," his father said, and he stopped. "Talk to no one."

The Storm Beyond the Tides

CHAPTER 2

ELLIE LAY ON THE SAND, EYES CLOSED, THE HOT SUN AGAINST her back. In the backdrop, she could hear the steady whoosh of the waves, children laughing, seagulls. Beyond that, the low hum of trawlers going through Taylor Passage and the gong of a channel marker.

"Can you believe those louses?"

She lifted one eye and saw Kate leaning on her elbows, staring at the spot where only a few minutes before a family had been. All that remained was an empty milk carton, cookie boxes, cigarette butts, and a dirty diaper.

"Maybe they'll be back?" she said.

But she didn't believe it, knowing it was the main reason locals hated tourists—they treated Monk Island like their own playground, renting cottages and leaving them in shambles, crowding the ferries and sidewalks.

"That's why I can't wait to leave this place."

"It that so," Ellie said with obvious bitterness.

"I don't mean it like that," Kate said, glancing back. "But wouldn't you like to see the world?"

Ellie thought back to high school when all they talked about was leaving Monk Island, going so far as to get maps from the library, books on travel, employment guides for major cities. But those dreams of youth were soon tempered by the reality of circumstances, and although Kate's parents could afford to send her to college, Ellie's could not.

"I've been applying for jobs in Portland," Ellie said.

"Would you ever move?"

"If the right opportunity came along."

Something caught Kate's attention and she paused, squinting towards the water.

"And maybe this is him."

When Ellie looked, she saw a young man strolling down the beach alone, arms at his side and looking around with timid curiosity. He was tall and lean, and with the glare of the sun, it took her a moment to realize it was the foreigner she had met in front of Lavery's.

"He asked me for directions a couple days ago."

"Did he?" Kate said, but she was more interested in gawking.

"He's from another country."

"Where?"

"Not sure."

"Maybe he's a prince," she went on. "I'd be his princess."

"Stop with such nonsense."

Ellie was just ready to lie back down when she heard, "we have a raft!" and turned to see Mary and June "Junebug" Mallet, Kate's sister, coming over the dunes. They looked like two waifs, windswept and sunburnt, with hand-me-down dresses and bare feet. Junebug was dragging something with a rope and Mary struggled to keep up with her crutches sinking in the sand.

"Where'd you get that?" Kate said.

"Somebody threw it out."

Ellie stood up and saw an inflated contraption with faded numbers on one side, German words she didn't understand. The rubber was split in places, but it was sturdy enough to hold air, and she was sure it was an old military raft. Twenty years on and keepsakes from the Great War were still emerging from the sheds and barns of Monk Island.

"Can we go to the sandbar?"

Mary glimpsed up pleading, her face scrunched, her tangled hair glistening. Ellie's first instinct was to say no, but she knew that her sister had to take some risks if she was ever going to be independent.

"Okay. Just to the sandbar."

Mary turned to Junebug and their faces beamed. They pulled the raft down to the water and Mary got in, putting her crutches over her lap. Junebug pushed them into the waves then hung onto the side kicking, and Ellie watched as they drifted towards the sandbar. Satisfied that they were safe, she leaned back, closed her eyes, and with the soothing sounds of the shore whirling around, sank into a drowsy semi-sleep.

Sometime later—a scream.

Realizing she had dozed, Ellie leaned up and scanned the water and saw splashing a hundred yards out.

"My God, Mary?!"

She ran down to the shore, Kate close behind, but stopped at the waterline because, like everyone in her family, she couldn't swim. People got up from their lounge chairs and towels, gravitated towards her, unsure what was happening.

"What's wrong, Dear?" one woman asked.

"Is everything alright?" said another.

The questions came fast and frantically, and Ellie was too panicked to answer. Kate threw down her hat and was just ready to go in when, from out of nowhere, the foreigner came sprinting down the beach. He splashed into the water, pointed his arms, and dove in, and Ellie's chest pounded as she watched, quietly praying and terrified beyond words. He swam towards the scene faster than she had ever seen anyone swim before and within seconds, he was halfway to the girls and closing in.

"He's got them," Kate said, gripping Ellie's arm.

The entire beach watched anxiously as the young man took the girls in his arms and the limp raft drifted away. With a slow and graceful backstroke, he returned to shore, and Ellie met him in the shallows to the applause of dozens of onlookers.

"This one's okay," he said, panting.

Junebug leaped out of his arms and plopped through the water to dry land.

"Mary," Ellie cried, pushing the wet bangs from her sister's face.

"She swallowed some water, I think."

The young man rushed Mary up to the beach and people gathered around. He flipped her over, tapped her a couple of times on the back, and she began to spit up seawater. Once she was empty, she coughed and took a few deep breaths, then looked up.

"My crutches sank."

There was nervous laughter all around and the young man grinned. Bystanders patted him on the back, praised him for his quick response —someone even used the word "hero." Ellie wiped a tear from her eye, put her arm around her sister, and they were both trembling.

Finally, she turned to the young man and their eyes met.

"Thank you so much. That was awful brave."

"It was nothing, really," he said with genuine modesty. "She's the brave one. But next time have a sturdier boat."

Hearing his accent again, she wondered where he was from, but before she could ask, a man came over and said, "Where'd you learn to swim like that, Son?"

"Back home, I used to swim, competitively."

"And where's that?"

He wavered, glanced around uncomfortably.

"Um, I am from...Germany."

As Ellie and Mary walked up the hill, Ellie saw her father standing in the shadow of the porch, his arms crossed, glaring. She could always feel his presence, whether he was a mile out to sea or at the far end of the beach, and she could tell his mood simply by his posture. On an island where everyone knew everybody else, news spread fast, and she was prepared to get scolded even before coming into the yard.

"Mary should NOT have been out there alone!"

Ellie stopped short on the walkway.

"Alone?" she said coldly. "She wasn't alone. She was with June."

Their mother burst out the front door, her hands waving, flustered.

"Darling. Are you alright?"

She met Mary on the steps and felt her forehead, looking her up and down, as fraught as any mother would be.

"She's fine, Mother," Ellie said. "She swallowed some seawater is all."

Vera put her arm around her daughter and took her inside. Before the door shut, Mary glanced back with a long face, as if to apologize, and Ellie smiled to let her know it wasn't her fault. And it wasn't. The differences between Ellie and her father were deeper than what happened at the beach, and her mother said they fought like Cain and Abel. Ellie knew he always wanted a son, and, in some ways, Jack found an adoptive heir in Ben Frazier, whom he mentored closely, teaching him all the finer points of lobstering. But it wasn't the same, and she often wondered if he resented her for being a woman.

They faced each other from a distance, Ellie in the yard and Jack on the porch. She hoped the silence would calm him, but the longer it went, the angrier he looked. With his boat still out of order, he hadn't worked since Tuesday, and she knew the idle time made him irritable.

"Mary shouldn't be in the water. She can't swim."

"Neither can you!"

Ellie could feel the tension rise like a change in atmospheric pressure. When she was a girl, one look from her father was enough to make her cower, shiver, repent. But she was an adult now and wouldn't be blamed when she hadn't done anything wrong. They all talked about giving Mary more freedom, but Jack seemed unwilling to let either of his daughters out from under his protective grasp. He was *damn domineering*, as Kate once said and, although Ellie was offended at the time, she realized later that her friend was right.

"Go down to Lavery's," he said, finally. "See if that belt came in."

Ellie consented with a quick, stubborn nod and her father went back into the house, leaving her alone and fuming.

She walked to the top of the street and turned onto Gull Avenue, a wide thoroughfare lined with ancient trees that curved down to the waterfront and into the village. In the cool of the shade, the effects of the argument faded and, as her mind wandered, she thought about the young man who had saved Mary.

There was something different about the German family—Ellie felt it the moment she saw them. All her life, she had watched tourists come off the ferry, wide-eyed and bursting with excitement, their hectic city lives behind them for a few weeks. But this family seemed much more somber, like they had just come from a funeral, and in their eyes, she saw a deep exhaustion that no amount of work or travel could produce.

By the time she got to Lavery's, the shop was closed but the door was still open. She walked in and Joe Mallet was in the corner, hunched over a crate, unpacking supplies from Portland. He always seemed to be at work, whether it was before dawn or late at night, and he tended to the shop like it was his child. Jack grumbled that Lavery's was a *license to print money*, and he always envied the Mallet's for having a business.

"Ellie," Joe Mallet said. "How's Mary? Kate told me what happened."

When he stood up, she heard his knees creak.

"She just swallowed some seawater. She'll be fine."

It was a response that, by now, was well-rehearsed, and she would have to repeat it until people stopped asking.

"Well, I'm glad to hear it. The belt arrived."

While he went into the back room, she stood quietly and looked around. She remembered when Kate's father bought the place before Mary and Junebug were born, and Jack helped install the original shelves, built the plywood counter. As young girls, she and Kate would spend hours in the shop on hot days, watching men come in with soiled bibs and wet boots, their faces crisp from the sun. Lavery's then was the center of the world, and Ellie once had the same fascination with boats, bobs, and buoys as Mary. But that was long ago, when the freshness of youth made everything seem new and important, even the day-to-day drudgery of lobstering.

"Ellie?"

She came out of the daydream and Joe was in front of her, holding out the belt.

"Yes, terrific, looks fine," she said, although she didn't know much about motors. "Would you please put it on his tab?"

He hesitated, squinting through his glasses, his expression concerned but kind. Ellie never asked her father about money, but the lobster industry had been struggling for almost a decade and many men had gone bust.

"Sure, Ellie, sure."

She thanked him with an awkward smile then took the belt and went to leave.

"Say, Ellie?..."

She stopped and turned around in dread, fearing that he was going to mention the tab. Even with no one else around, it was a humiliating topic.

"...with Kate leaving, I'll be looking for help if you're interested?"

The relief she felt was bittersweet because, like many locals, Joe Mallet knew that she had graduated in May and still didn't have a job.

"I'd have to check with Father...it being the busy season and all."

"Well, let me know."

"I will. Thank you," she said and walked out.

Somedays Ellie felt like the entire community was waiting to see what she would do with her life. She had applied for several positions in Portland, mostly bookkeeping and secretarial work, but she had yet to receive a single offer. Her father always claimed that mainlanders were prejudiced against islanders, a myth that everyone in his generation clung to. Like any two places so closely linked by culture and economics, there was a long history of tension, disputes, suspicion, and one-upman-ship. But the world had changed since Jack was a boy, and the Great War did much to upend the Yankee tribalism of the past. Ellie found it hard to believe that anyone in the city cared enough about Monk Islanders to despise them.

Outside the wind had shifted to the east and the sun was almost down, immersing the village in a dusky twilight. By now, the crowds had dwindled to a few random couples browsing the windows of the closed shops, relaxing on benches. Down at the terminal, a ferry was idling and passengers were lined up at the gate, waiting for the deckhands to finish unloading the cargo so they could board.

As she crossed the street, she heard a loud rumble and saw two Army trucks roll off the ramp and come up the hill. It was an unusual sight in peacetime, but Monk Island was no stranger to the military and, because of its location, it had always been part of the Portland Harbor defense system. During the Great War, the Army built a bunker and generator building on the eastern side of the island where, as a child, Ellie and her friends would play among its abandoned ramparts.

The trucks stopped at the intersection and a young soldier looked over, his helmet low, his expression stern. They locked eyes for a moment, then the driver put it in gear, cut right, and sped off down Gull Avenue, and Ellie watched as they went around the bend and vanished in the shadows.

Everyone knew about the political troubles around the world, and, in high school, Ellie's class had followed events in real-time, from the war in Spain to the Japanese invasion of China to the rise of Adolph Hitler. For most of her peers, the chaos beyond was as significant as the stars, astonishing but of no consequence on the remote shores of Maine. The older generation that lived through the First World War was warier, however, and people grumbled about how, if America got pulled into another one, it might not have the luxury of fighting it somewhere else. Jack had mentioned the possibility of the country being attacked— although never in front of Mary—and Joe Mallet did too. As Ellie stood thinking, the stench of the truck exhaust still in the air, she realized that the world was changing fast, and for the first time, she was worried about the future.

∼

Purchase your copy now!

https://www.amazon.com/dp/B09BM419DK

Like Audio Books? Listen to *The Storm Beyond the Tides* for **free** on Audible!

https://ltryan.ink/FLD9

Bermuda Blue

∼

CHAPTER 1

The war had been over for almost a year, but for Jerry Canavan some days it felt like it just ended. When he returned from Europe the previous September, it was as if he had been dropped back into society from a nightmare. He moved home with his parents, the small but familiar apartment he had grown up in. While he was away, his older sister Ellen had gotten married and moved to Rhode Island with her new husband, who worked for a tugboat company and had avoided the draft because his job was a "reserved occupation." His sister Patricia, who was eight years younger, had graduated high school and was living in Beacon Hill with roommates, where she studied nursing during the day and worked as a switchboard operator by night.

At first, things seemed very much the same with only a few minor exceptions. The Lovells across the street had painted their house; next door, one of the two dachshunds had died from tapeworms, although Jerry wasn't sure which because they were twins. The O'Connor children—Robby and Patrice—who were barely teenagers when Jerry left for the service, were now young adults. A black family had bought the house at the corner, something that more than one person had casually mentioned. Jerry's mother still rose before dawn to feed the birds, his father getting up shortly after to have coffee and toast before walking the five blocks to his job at the post office. And finally, Ray Joyce, an only child who lived three doors down, had been killed at Guadalcanal, leaving his parents in a state of permanent mourning where they only left the house to go to church. As much as Jerry had hoped to return to the safe and predictable life he had left three years before, he couldn't escape the fact that the world had changed.

Those first weeks back were the hardest. He slept in late and spent his weekends at the local VFW post, where old veterans mingled with the hordes of young men still pouring back from overseas. There he saw people he had known all his life, sharing stories about the places they had been and the things they had seen, a mix of memories both poignant and painful. It felt more like a long wake than a reunion, however, because not a day went by that he didn't learn about some neighborhood friend or acquaintance who had died. And despite all the pride and bravado that went along with being victors, they had all lost some part of themselves they would never get back.

With a letter of introduction from a college friend, Jerry got an interview at the Boston Globe, and to his surprise, they hired him as a cub reporter. Journalism was never a career he planned, but an intern-ship with the school newspaper *The Heights* at Boston College had led to him becoming assistant editor by senior year. So he got his first real job, and although it wasn't glamorous, it at least gave him the comfort and normalcy of a daily routine.

He had spent most of that winter covering local events, from high school basketball tournaments to the arrival of Liberty ships, which six months after the war's end were still bringing troops and equipment back from Europe. He was drinking too much, and he knew it, but since coming back he experienced a paralyzing irritability that only a half pint of Old Crow seemed to soothe. His parents were the first to notice, although he never drank at home, and his father's only advice, conveyed one night during the radio intermission of *The Lone Ranger,* was to stick to beer.

Jerry stayed dry for weeks at a time, more out of stubbornness than desire. But the days were drudgery, the passion gone from his spirit, the world a dull and pointless slog. His mother said it was *war neurosis*, something she had read about in a women's magazine—his father said he needed to have more milk. When Jerry showed up drunk to a Red Cross food drive, someone told his supervisor who, as a veteran of the Great War, was more than sympathetic. Instead of reprimanding him, he offered Jerry the chance to fly down and cover the Newport Bermuda yacht race, which after a six-year hiatus during the war, was finally back on. It was a *chance to relax*, his boss told him, and Jerry accepted the assignment, hoping that maybe the sun and sand might be the cure for his malaise.

~

The plane touched down with a thud, jolting Jerry from his daydream. He wiped some condensation off the window and looked out, where he saw palm trees, white-roofed homes, and low hills nestled into a landscape of a thousand shades of green. In the distance, the last glints of sun faded over the horizon, casting a soft and dusky haze over everything.

The cabin door opened, bringing in a rush of warm, moist air and the sweet smell of tropical vegetation. Jerry reached for his duffel bag and headed down the aisle, smiling at the few scattered passengers. The flight was only half full, mostly older couples and retirees, men with light-colored suits and hats and women wearing flowered dresses. But there were families too, and Jerry always liked to see children because they made him think of the future.

He continued down the gangway and onto the tarmac, which reeked of oil and, even at sunset, still radiated heat like an oven. There were military trucks everywhere. At the end of the runway, he saw the sandbags of a checkpoint, and the sight of soldiers standing around with rifles made him quietly uneasy. Beside a hangar, he saw a row of P-51 Mustangs, parked at an angle like they were ready for battle. Throughout the war, Kindley Field had been an Army airbase, but now it was a mix of commercial and military use. Tourism may have been on the rebound, Jerry thought, but it still looked like a military compound.

He walked into the terminal, where a proper black man with glasses took his passport and stamped it.

"Welcome to Bermuda," he said with a lilting island accent.

Jerry smiled and continued through a set of double doors, stopping as he walked outside. Standing in front of him and leaning against a blue British convertible was Cam. He posed like a lifestyle model for Harper's Bazaar, with linen pants and sandals, a sweater tied around his shoulders. The car was no less elegant, its long running boards and rounded chrome grille gleaming against the dry and dusty dullness of the airport access road.

With a deep grin, Cam took a drag on his cigarette and flicked it, his gold watch rattling. He blew out the smoke and stared at Jerry for close to a minute before speaking.

"You made it," he said.

Considering all they had been through, the remark could have meant many things, and Cam seemed to know it. But Jerry was too tired for a long and poignant reunion, so he just walked over, put down his bag, and they embraced.

"Good to see you, Cam," he said, then stepped back and looked his friend up and down. "You look terrific."

"And you look like hell."

Jerry laughed out loud, and he needed some humor.

"Probably because I've been through it," he said.

"We'll get to that. First, let's get you into town for a welcome aperitif. You look right parched."

Jerry smiled hesitantly. It was a conversation he had dreaded, but he was eager to get it over with.

"I...I really can't," he said.

"Can't? What's *can't*?"

"I'm dry."

"My God," Cam said, and he looked truly confused. "No hooch?"

"Not a drop. Doctor's orders."

Jerry had planned the story weeks before, knowing that if he didn't have a good excuse, Cam would only continue to hound him. And he wouldn't have begrudged him for it because much of their years of fun and friendship in college had revolved around drinking.

Cam thought for a moment, clearly disappointed, then with a quiet acceptance, he reached down for Jerry's bag and tossed it in the backseat.

"I'd expect that sort of condemnation from a judge, not a physician," he muttered.

When he opened the passenger door, Jerry looked around before getting in. Aside from a bus, there were no other civilian vehicles, and the small line of taxis waiting by the entrance were all horse buggies.

"Go on," Cam urged him. "It doesn't bite."

Jerry sat in the bucket seat, the leather smooth and unblemished, the cushions so soft they felt like pillows. Cam walked around and got in, nodding to some tourists who were gazing at the car. He turned the key and the engine sputtered to life, a low, powerful rumble like the snore of a sleeping bear.

"What kinda car is this?" Jerry asked, looking at the walnut dashboard.

"'43 Morgan Roadster," he said proudly, as he lit another Chesterfield cigarette.

When he held out the pack, Jerry declined, continuing the conversation so he didn't have to explain that he had given up smoking too.

"It's yours?" he asked.

"Indeed. Are you surprised?"

"Where'd you get it?"

Cam leaned back, one hand on the wheel, and turned to him with a mischievous grin.

"A long story, old friend," he said.

Putting it in gear, he revved the engine, and Jerry fell back in the seat as they sped off.

"I don't doubt it."

Bermuda Blue

~

CHAPTER 2

TALL, BLONDE, AND HANDSOME, CAMERON "CAM" MCSHANE was like the poster boy for the American dream. He was the robust and overachieving son of equally overachieving parents, and Jerry wondered how the hell they ever became such good friends. They met the first day at Boston College in '38 when Cam walked into class wearing the shirt from an intramural Boston hockey league which they both had, at different times, played for. With penny loafers and houndstooth trousers, his impeccable hair parted to one side, he looked more suited to the sailing club than hockey, and Jerry was surprised to find out that he was one tough football player. Cam was the only person who called him "Jer," and the only thing Jerry knew about that mysterious world of prep schools and ski camps was that everyone had a nickname.

Cam's father owned the largest home heating oil delivery service in Boston, a business that his Irish great-grandfather originally started as a coal company. His mother was from a distinguished Bermudian family and had come to Boston after the First World War to attend B.U. Law School with the intention of becoming a patent attorney—or was it estate planning? Cam's family was successful in so many areas that Jerry couldn't keep track of their accomplishments.

Cam's parents met at a gala for the Appalachian Mountain Club in

Beacon Hill, an institution that, as Cam once put it, was like having a Mars society on Venus. Because his mother was Episcopalian and his father was not, the relationship was shrouded in all the petty class scandal of the era. Nevertheless, they married and produced two sons, Cam and his younger brother Bryce, both of whom his mother chose to stay at home and raise. The boys followed the predictable path of Boston's well-to-do Catholics: parochial grammar school, Boston College High School, and finally, Boston College.

Considering his pedigree, Cam always seemed to get what he wanted, which explained why, on an island where automobile ownership was strictly limited, he was driving a luxury car. His father had a friend who was a major at Fort Bell, and the man agreed to classify the Morgan as an "essential vehicle" as long as the Army could use it from time to time to entertain high-ranking officers or dignitaries. But like everything with Cam, there was a catch, and the story of how he came to own it was almost as impressive as the vehicle itself.

While Jerry had been in heavy combat, Cam spent the war at a remote joint U.S./UK training base near Glasgow, Scotland. There he got involved with the daughter of an aging aristocrat whose fortune had been squandered over the centuries, leaving the family with a manor house, some valuable land, and not much else. The girl was already engaged, her fiancé fighting with the Royal Scots in Burma, and when her father learned about the affair with Cam, he was outraged. He complained to Army officials, but fraternizing with locals wasn't prohibited, and the girl claimed she loved him.

When Cam got transferred to Surrey in late '44, the girl offered him her fiancé's car, some small token of her affection and maybe even a little insurance. But in wartime, nothing was certain. The young man was killed in battle, and her relationship with Cam fizzled out. In her last letter, she took back her heart but gave him the car. With the war in Europe fast coming to an end, there was just enough logistical chaos for Cam to convince an old college buddy in the Navy to slip the Morgan in with a shipment of jeeps that were headed for Bermuda. That was how Cam's life was, Jerry thought, a series of mishaps that always seemed to end up in his favor.

~

"Did you ever talk to her again?" Jerry asked.

"You can only love a woman once."

"That's not what I asked."

Cam glanced over with a smile, his expression a vague mix of indifference and regret.

"No," he said.

They turned down a narrow lane that was more like a footpath than a road, the hedgerows so high that, at some points, they blocked out the sky and the stars. Jerry could see a few lights, but most of the homes were hidden behind pink and white walls, obscured by thick vegetation.

Cam pulled into a driveway, the tires crunching over seashell gravel, and they stopped.

"We have arrived," he said.

"Nice digs."

The stucco house wasn't huge, but it was elegant, with round columns, copper gutters, and a stepped limestone roof that hung over the entrance. A flower garden ran the width of the front, and the smell of roses, lilies, and flowering hibiscus filled the air. It was dead quiet, the only sound the faint but constant hum of insects, the distant whoosh of the waves.

Jerry climbed out and stretched his arms with a big yawn. After a long day of travel, his body ached all over, and he didn't know if he had been working too much lately or if he was just getting old.

"Tired, my friend?"

He looked over, and Cam was leaning against the car, his legs crossed, the tip of his cigarette glowing.

"I don't sleep like I used to," he said.

"None of us do."

Jerry raised his eyes, and although tempted to say something sarcastic, he didn't want to start off on the wrong foot. Cam didn't have the most dangerous post in the war, but it wasn't a competition. Both their lives had been altered, and they both lost friends. Myles Duggan, the star receiver at Boston College, was killed in Guadalcanal, and the junior varsity baseball team lost two players.

Jerry got his bag out of the back and threw it over his shoulder. As he started towards the front door, he stopped when he noticed Cam wasn't following.

"Wrong way," Cam said, flicking his cigarette.

"What?"

"You're staying in the pool house. It's more private."

"Lead the charge," Jerry said.

They walked down the side of the house and came out to the back, where a second-story balcony overlooked an in-ground pool. The property continued for another twenty yards, sloping down to the water in a manicured stretch of green grass and ending at a small, secluded cove. Just offshore, a half-dozen sailboats, mostly sloops, rocked gently in the calm evening tide.

Jerry followed Cam around the patio, and as they approached the pool house, he was relieved to see it was more like a small cottage than a shed. Cam opened the door, reached for the wall switch, and waved for him to enter. Inside was a single room with a kitchenette and a bathroom no bigger than a broom closet. Along the far wall was a twin bed and a window that faced the shore. There was a wooden chair, a small writing desk, and a Philco console in the corner. A few watercolor paintings hung from rusty nails, scenes of unpaved country lanes and sandy inlets, but otherwise, the décor was plain.

"So, what do you think?" Cam asked.

Jerry dropped his bag and looked around, mainly for show because, at this point, he would have slept in a doghouse.

"It's perfect."

When he got the assignment to Bermuda, the first thing he had done was send a letter to Cam, who wrote back inviting him to stay at his "estate." The accommodations weren't entirely what he expected, but he always did like privacy, and he would need it to work.

Jerry made a quick inspection of the room then turned to Cam, who stood looming in the doorway, his hair slicked back, his face damp from the heat.

"How 'bout I make some coffee?" he asked.

Cam made a tight, regretful smile.

"Thanks, but a lady awaits me in Somerset."

"A girlfriend?"

"You've been in Boston for too long, my friend," he said, shaking his head. "The word here is paramour, and it's never just one."

Jerry responded with a chuckle, neither surprised nor particularly impressed because Cam had always been a ladies' man.

"There're some biscuits in the cabinet," Cam went on. "Eggs and milk in the icebox. If you need anything in the AM, give me a holler. But I must warn you, I'm a late riser."

Jerry dropped his bag to the floor and sat on the bed, the mattress stiff but good enough.

"I won't bother you," he said.

"No bother. The rear door is always open. Kitchen is just upstairs to the right."

"Got it."

"Now, get some rest."

As he turned to go, Jerry called to him and Cam stopped. In the dim light of the small room, their eyes met, and the only reason Jerry hesitated was because he didn't know what to say, only that he had the urge to say something. So much had happened since they last saw each other, both personally and in the world, and between them lay the great, unspoken gulf of their interrupted lives. It would have been easier to pretend the war never happened, that after college they had both moved on and found careers and happiness. It was something that seemed to work at home where, after an emotional welcome and some obligatory questions, Jerry's parents never asked about his service, and he never brought it up.

Cam remained still, paused in the entrance with one hand on the knob. In the brief silence, Jerry found himself getting choked up, and he had never been one to cry easily or wallow in the sentimental. But he was moved enough that he was afraid to speak. Some part of him hoped that if he waited long enough, it would force Cam to talk first. And it did.

"What is it, Jer?" he asked, his voice low, gentle.

"I...I just wanted to say *thanks*."

Cam pressed his lips together and looked down, and Jerry was sure he heard a faint sigh. Although he didn't reply, his expression said more than any words could, and Jerry was satisfied in knowing he wasn't alone in those hidden feelings of emptiness, loss, and regret. With an awkward smile, Cam made a quick nod then retreated into the darkness, pulling the door shut behind him.

Purchase your copy now!

https://www.amazon.com/dp/B09L5DW67C

Also by Jonathan Cullen

The Days of War Series

The Last Happy Summer

Nighttime Passes, Morning Comes

Onward to Eden (Coming Soon)

Shadows of Our Time Collection

The Storm Beyond the Tides

Sunsets Never Wait

Bermuda Blue

The Jody Brae Mystery Series

Whiskey Point

City of Small Kingdoms

The Polish Triangle

Love Ain't For Keeping (Coming Soon)

Sign up for Jonathan's newsletter for updates on deals and new releases!

https://liquidmind.media/j-cullen-newsletter-sign-up-1/

About the Author

Jonathan Cullen grew up in Boston and attended public schools. After a brief career as a bicycle messenger, he graduated from Boston College with a B.A. in English Literature (1995). During his twenties, he wrote two unpublished novels, taught high school in Ireland, lived in Mexico, worked as a prison librarian, and spent a month in Kenya, Africa before finally settling down three blocks from where he grew up.

He currently lives in Boston (West Roxbury) with his wife Heidi and daughter Maeve.

Made in the USA
Middletown, DE
01 July 2024

56667285R00113